Bothayna Al-Essa is a bestselling ar
author. She has published nine novels
essays, children's books, and translation:
She lives in Kuwait.

All That I Want to Forget was published in A~~~~~~~ with the title
Kabirtu wa nasay~~~~~~~~~~~~~.

Michele Henjum is a translator with an MA in comparative literature. She lives in Cairo.

All That I Want to Forget

Bothayna Al-Essa

Translated by
Michele Henjum

منحة الترجمة
Translation Grant
صندوق منحة الشارقة للترجمة
Sharjah Translation Grant Fund

hoopoe
AN IMPRINT OF AUC PRESS

First published in 2019 by
Hoopoe
113 Sharia Kasr el Aini, Cairo, Egypt
200 Park Ave., Suite 1700 New York, NY 10166
www.hoopoefiction.com

Hoopoe is an imprint of the American University in Cairo Press
www.aucpress.com

Dar el Kutub No. 13355/18
ISBN 978 977 416 908 3

Dar el Kutub Cataloging-in-Publication Data

Al-Essa, Bothayna
        All That I Want to Forget / Bothayna Al-Essa.— Cairo: The American
University in Cairo Press, 2018.
        p.   cm.
        ISBN 978 977 416 908 3
        1.   English Fiction
        832

1 2 3 4 5   23 22 21 20 19

Designed by Adam el-Sehemy
Printed in the United States of America

For N

You should never be here too much; be so far away that they can't find you, they can't get at you to shape, to mould. Be so far away, like the mountains, like the unpolluted air; be so far away that you have no parents, no relations, no family, no country; be so far away that you don't know even where you are. Don't let them find you; don't come into contact with them too closely. Keep far away where even you can't find yourself . . .

—*J. Krishnamurti*

Do not go far away, they say, as they bury me.
Where is far away if not where I am?

—*Malik Ibn al-Rayb*

I Grew Up

They always told me, *You'll grow up and forget all about it.*

When I fell and cracked my skull.
When my math teacher told me to stand facing the wall,
Because I forgot that 7 x 6 = 42.

When my bicycle broke and they didn't buy me another,
So I wouldn't break it.
When the vessel sheltering my spirit broke.

When my parents died.
When I didn't die.
When the world was too much and I was alone.

When my brother tore apart my doll because Barbie is haram,
And canceled Spacetoon because Pokémon is haram.

When he removed the photograph of my mother and father
from the picture frame and buried it in the broken drawer,
So as not to drive the angels away.

When the cracks in the wall filled with devils.

When I was forced to enroll in the Girls' College,
To preserve my chastity.

When he offered me to his friend in marriage,
To preserve my chastity.

When I tore the covers off my books to protect them from
the fire.
When I wrote my first poem on the bottom of a box of tissues,
Trembling in fear.

When he dragged me by my hijab at my first poetry reading.
When he finally slapped me.

They all said, *You'll grow up and forget all about it.*

Problem is, I grew up and didn't forget.
I grew up and I didn't forget all that I want to forget.

Eating the Apple

"Mirror, mirror on the wall,
Who's the ugliest one of all?"

"You are, O apple eater.
You are, O naughty bookworm.
You are."

I DIDN'T WAKE UP, I plummeted to awareness.

The mirror in front of me, terror filling my pores.

Who am I?

The dream had thrown me out. It wasn't a nice dream, though I'd have preferred to continue it rather than return to this place. For a moment I wondered, what's this? Where am I? Then I realized—or remembered. This is where I'm hiding. I'm in the hotel. I ran away. It wasn't yet 3:30 a.m. What was I going to do with myself, awake? I bent my knees and pulled them to my stomach, hugging myself. I'm a ball in the form of a woman, more ball than woman. Like a letter C with its wrists tied together.

I pulled the blanket over my head and closed my eyes. Sleep, Fatima. Tomorrow we'll sort out your thoughts. Tomorrow you'll iron your shirt and comb your hair and sort out your thoughts. That's the plan. All you have to do now is sleep. The night isn't on your side. You know that, Fatima, and still you wake like this.

3

I curled up into myself, a snail that knew what to do. Sleep, little one, sleep. I sang to myself as if I were my mother, as if I were my child, as if I were the only person I had left, because I was the only person I had left. My limbs were trembling, my body was in revolt. The dreadful reality washed over me like the horror that always accompanies that simple question. Who am I? I ran away. You really ran away, Fatima.

The face in the mirror mocked me. Shout it out, Archimedes, shout out your brilliant discovery. Wake the whole world up! Please sleep, Fatima. Go to sleep, quick, before the outlines of the story come back, the immorality and indecency of it all, its power over you. Before the thought absorbs you entirely and sucks the life out of you, leaving you withered and powerless.

I can't stop thinking. I have to turn off this crazy machine they call the mind. I jump out of bed, my fingers shaking as I open my suitcases, my fingers as frantic as I am, bony and sweaty and injured like me. I open the suitcases one after the other, tear through them, throwing things out, rummaging and raging through them, ransacking the contents. I dig my fingers deep, deep into the pockets and openings and corners of the suitcases. I dive, searching for relief, for that damn bottle of pills that pulls me gently out of my reality. Alprazolam, the magical soporific, cure for epilepsy, anxiety, and depression—my best friend and worst enemy, working steadily, with my blessing, toward my undoing.

Where are they, those little devils? Come, dears. Come, little ones. Come, before I run out of the room and turn myself in to the first policeman or tissue vendor I find in the street. I fumble over the bottle under the cotton pajamas. Opening it with trembling fingers, I swallow a pill. I assure the frantic being inside me that things are under control. Calm down, Fatima. You took the medicine.

I am sinking into the bed. The bed is a pit and I fall. The pit is endless, like bloodshed, like the hungry, like the dead, like Sayyab's poetry: "Your gifts, my Lord, I accept them all.

4

Bring them . . . Bring them . . . O giver of shells and death."
Am I delirious? I'm shaking, and not from passion or ecstasy
or prophetic revelation. The alprazolam is tearing through
me, leaving me lit. A terrible dryness in my mouth. There's no
water in the well.

I close my eyes and see Faris. He's searching for me
through the many streets, wandering the sidewalks and looking all over, looking for me behind trees and under rocks. I
smile at him tenderly and mumble with a tongue thick as a
bag of sand, *Sleep, dear. Sleep.* The numbness crawls toward me
from my fingertips, my limbs are shrinking. I'm slowly being
eaten away, getting smaller and smaller. I grow numb and can
now think of Faris. I feel sorry for him. With my weak throat
and thin voice, I sing to him, sing him to sleep.

Prayer

I embrace the shattered pieces of myself so that I
might write.
Inside I am destroyed.
Show me Your might, O Almighty.

Teach me to pray,
A prayer of my own.
Give me my language.

Give me my language, O Lord of Language.
Give me my language so that I might pray to You,
To You the honor and the glory.

Give me all of my words.
Give me my language so that I might think, so that I
might exist,
So that I might know myself, so that I might know You.

LORD OF CLARITY, CREATOR OF MAN, be with me in my solitude, for I am lost in the underground tombs. I want a word
that I might set afire, that might set me afire. A word that I
might return to life, that might return me to life. A word from
which I might draw warmth and illuminate what is inside me.

The word that was in the beginning. The word that created
the world out of nothing. The word that brought me here, to

this place. I make out my prayers with the tips of my fingers; I can sense the letters with my heart. Give me the word, the secret word, the secret of truth, the truth of wisdom. Give me the wisdom to forgive this loss. Give me my language.

Give me the first letter of the answer so that I might understand the ugliness of the world, so that I might make sense of the harm and forgive. Give me L so that I might love, C so that I might contain and find compassion. I am drained of life, and water is hard to find. I am parched and far from myself. Give me D so that I might depart, might disappear. Give me R so that I might rest, might relax, might recover and find a way to heal. Give me S, give me T, give me U and V and W. Give me my language so that I might cultivate this wasteland called my life, so that I might illuminate the tomb inhabited by the ghosts and devils crouching deep in the caves of memory. Give me F so that I might forget, might feel, might flourish like a tree. Give me language, O Lord of Language, to You the honor and the power and the glory, on earth as in heaven. I am small and weak and insignificant, and this vast creation shall be yours forever and ever.

Give me my language.

A Withered Old Woman

It's an ideal place for one to be unseen,
For a woman to be unseen.

A ROOM FOR TWENTY-FIVE dinars a night, in a cheap hotel that
flaunts its ugliness as if it were an achievement. In the shad-
ows of the mongrel crowds of Salmiya, among a group of
sluggish cafés propped against each other as if holding themselves up, the cafés' patrons spread out along the sidewalk next
to the red coals of their nargilehs, enveloped by the thick scent
of grilled meat and sitting under a turban of smoke.

I melt into the throng and nearly disappear.

I have no odor and no shadow.

I am no one.

I am in the right place. Not just because no one would expect
to find me here, but because the place resembles me—its
unforgivable lack of shame, already old despite its youth, a
pond of fish gutted by grief. The blue curtains, the burgundy
sofas, the scandalous absence of any harmony among its
parts—everything here is me.

I feel I've lost many limbs crossing the miles. Emptiness
has left its stains on me. I have died and buried myself many
times, and have nowhere left inside that is green and alive. I
am an old woman at twenty-five, a withered old woman.

When I talk about why I ran away I have to be convincing. I can't come across like a crazy woman addicted to pills, a poet railing against the dryness and distance of things. It's easy to condemn me; I need to make things clear, quantifiable, with sharp edges, simple as a percentage. The answer was to run. The data is endless and the story isn't a straight line, but I will try anyway.

I want Faris to understand that I couldn't stay in that world a moment longer. A world of coffins and tombs. A world of shoes that walk all over me. I want to eliminate all possible ties to the conventional way of life. I want chaos—to sleep when I want and eat as I want, to be silent as much as I want. I want to want. I am starved for my will, starved for myself. I hunger to feel, for the first time in my life, that I am immune to violation, that no one's claws will rip away the shield masking my frailty.

I've started to understand that it's pointless for me to think about our marriage, and our impending divorce, as isolated from the seven years I spent in that basement. That is what I tried, and failed, to tell Faris: you married an old woman of twenty. They stole many years; years that I was supposed to live, innocent and youthful. I can't be your wife; nothing will grow here.

I'll stay here. I'll hide here my entire life, with my bottle of alprazolam, my socks, my glass vases stuffed with papers, my computer. Here in the hotel flaunting its three stars, celebrating its perpetual inferiority, and delighted by its truth. I'll stay here on the second floor, room twenty-eight, and write.

The Tomb

I Didn't Cry at My First Funeral

IT WASN'T THE FIRST TIME.

The first time I snuck out of the house I was nineteen years old. It was unplanned and careless. Life was a mess so I went out, and called going out "running away." Then I called running away "salvation," and salvation "death." I said I won't go back no matter what. I'd only go back as a body.

I drove the black Subaru to the nearest Burger King and bought a super-sized Double Whopper. I wanted everything to be huge, greasy, and excessive. I paid, took the paper bag in one hand and the bucket of Pepsi in the other, and crossed the street to the girls' high school that I'd graduated from two years earlier. I crouched in front of the entrance and started eating.

It was in exactly this spot that I used to stand after school every day, waiting for my older brother to arrive, famished and dying to eat something. I'd inhale the greasy smell of fried food and think about french fries.

Getting to the other side of the street seemed impossible given the school's tight security. The school counselor would wait until the last student left before going home, her conscience clear. She had made it her duty in life to make sure we didn't cross those few meters to the restaurant unaccompanied by our "guardian."

The girls who were braver than me, who dared violate the sacred and shatter taboos for the sake of a Whopper meal or a Chicken Royale, those intrepid girls, fully in tune with their desires, were taught a lesson the next day, forced to stand in the middle of the schoolyard during lineup, where we all witnessed what I called the "three-minute roar," because the principal's voice went beyond mere yelling. It was perfectly humiliating, and delivered in such a manner as to produce a "story" from which we'd take away the moral and our lesson on the fate of wayward girls embroiled by desire.

Why didn't we just wait for our guardians then? Because the driver isn't considered a guardian. Because guardians would never permit their daughters to eat outside the home when the table there was overflowing with platters of rice and rich meaty sauces. Because there is pleasure in the forbidden.

The public humiliation hadn't scared me, and I wouldn't have minded the principal's verbal beating, or the scandal of the public punishment in lineup, as much as I feared my brother would find out about it and the octopod arms of the school's punishment would reach into my home. In those years I was convinced that bad deeds were rewarded ten times over, and good deeds were worthless.

Four years and I didn't cross. I never gave in. I abandoned the voice inside me and just stood there, the sun boring into my head, eating the Whopper in my imagination—picking it up in my hands, tasting it, hot and juicy in my mouth.

That day, the first time I ran away, I purchased my forbidden fruit and sat with my back to the school entrance and ate. Screw the principal and the teachers and my big brother. I had my revenge.

I finished the mountain of rubbery American food within minutes, half in attempt to smother my fears. I grew heavier and calmer. I walked back to the car parked in front of the restaurant, wondering, now what? The food I'd eaten suddenly heaved in my stomach, then came up fiery and acidic. My cheeks were hot and my eyes burned with tears. I wiped my mouth with the napkins and paper bags in my hand and sobbed. Why had the forbidden fruit I'd craved for so long rejected me?

It had been a year since I'd gotten my driver's license and I wasn't familiar with the streets. The Subaru was the driver's car; they'd notice it was gone any moment now. I was afraid I might get lost, but I was more afraid that my failed attempt to run away would become a scandal. Had I been serious about leaving, things wouldn't have happened so randomly, without a suitcase or money or even a passport.

The horizons collapsed before me. I kept driving forward, forward, always forward, sobbing. I knew I was fooling myself, but going back to that place, that house, that tomb—I wished for a moment that a car would hit me and I'd die and it'd be all over. Then I figured out the solution.

If I really died, all of my problems would be over. If I surrendered to death, getting through the rest of my days wouldn't be this hard. I'd deal with things like a corpse. My death would be thick, and the world wouldn't be able to get through.

I took the Fourth Ring Road to Jabriya. I turned right and continued until I got to a flower shop. Since I only had three dinars left after the super-sized lunch I'd eaten and vomited back up in a half hour, I bought the cheapest flowers: a bunch of day-old white daisies, simple and starting to smell bad. I drove to the Jabriya public garden, empty except for some Asians and Syrian families eating sandwiches on blankets they'd spread out on the grass. I walked in a straight line, as though following a secret call. I searched for the right gravesite, someplace appropriate for me and my symbolic death. While walking, I cursed my uncomfortable shoes and rash decisions. In the sandy space between two cactuses, I dug a hole and buried the white flower petals in it. I decided that I'd died, and called that spot my grave. I'd died and found peace and it was all over.

I didn't cry at my first funeral. I thought, if somehow they found out about my death they wouldn't have cried either. I had a strange feeling of relief as I finished my ceremonial burial. I wouldn't feel any more pain now, because I was dead.

I went home. No one had found out that I'd snuck out, or returned, or that I'd died. For them, nothing had happened. But I knew that the part of me that had died, that I'd buried between the cactuses without tears or fanfare, was something I'd never get back.

The Pit

THE CAR ROLLED OVER AND with it the whole world.

The story could begin here. With the accident, when reality acquired teeth. I was in my pink pajamas, dipping french fries in chili sauce and watching television. I was thirteen and death had forgotten me.

Everything had been fine. Then the grown-ups started whispering, drying their tears with their sleeves and hugging each other, exchanging the news of my parents' death as quietly as possible. I was still dipping my fingers in the chili sauce and licking it off, as if the disaster hadn't happened. What was wrong with them? Why was everyone coming over to our house and crying? Why were they whispering like that? I went to see, crept over and hid behind the half-open door, strained to hear. I learned some new words: corpses, corpse washer, quick death, Arar Road. I heard people saying, *"There is no power and no strength save in God."* I heard a lot of sighing and sniffling and tissues being pulled from boxes. I hadn't known, yet, that the disaster concerned me more than it did them.

When my uncle's wife came to close the door she saw me behind it and let out a sob. For a moment I thought she was going to scold me for eavesdropping, but when she saw me she put her hand on her mouth and cried, Oh sweet little Fatima! Just like that, for no reason. I froze, looking at them, hearing things that meant nothing. Does she know? No. What are you waiting for? We're waiting for Saqr. God help them. One of

17

my relatives asked me to go upstairs with her. Why? I want to watch the adults cry and fall apart. Come, Fatima, let's go play. Do you have any toys you can show me? She was crazy, this woman. Did she think I was five years old?

Then Saqr arrived, my half brother, my big brother, sixteen years older, square and stocky, with huge hands, a red face, and a thick beard, the number eleven between his eyes and three lines curving across his forehead. My uncles hugged him. Our deepest sympathies. May he rest in peace. God have mercy on your father. Dad? I asked. Dad died? Their faces clenched in tears that almost fell on my face. Saqr leaned over, looked at me with his red eyes. Your father and your mother, Fatima. Say, May they rest in peace. Mom too? May she rest in peace. Mom and Dad? May they rest in peace. May they rest in peace?

I fell into the pit. The pit I fell into is in me, the pit is me, the fall is me, the endless falling. I kicked. I punched my fists. Saqr hugged me tightly, said, Shhhh. There, there. Don't be afraid, I won't leave you. You'll come with me. I'll take care of you.

Yes. He'll take excellent care of me. I'll become his greatest concern; he'll take care of me so well I'll crumble, from the inside out.

Wedding-Night Pajamas

THE NIGHT OF MY WEDDING I went to bed wearing ridiculous cotton pajamas: blue pants flecked with white and a white top with a smiling and winking yellow tulip in the middle. Ridiculous and comfortable pajamas that served their purpose. Pajamas that said, "Don't think about touching me!"

I had no interest in getting to know the man who had become my husband, or to ease his fright over the way our wedding had been conducted, with my brother's thick hand pushing me toward him with barely a congratulations.

As the cars parked in rows outside the house, the guests thought perhaps they had the wrong place. Where were the drums and the guests? they wondered. Where were the ululations? Where were the festive lights? The Sri Lankan maid opened the door and waved them inside to the sitting room. There sat Faris with his mom, two sisters, five aunts, and a few female cousins, waiting for the "celebration" to begin. His mom, seeking reassurance, asked, Is it today? Everyone searched themselves and their mobiles for the date. His sisters were annoyed with their skyscraper-high hairdos; were annoyed as well with the joke of calling this a celebration, given the screaming indifference of the residents of the house, our house. After a few minutes Wadha went downstairs and told them the bride was still getting ready. After a few more minutes Badriya entered, covered in her abaya, and asked Faris to sit in the salon because Saqr would meet him there in a few minutes.

It wasn't a few minutes. Faris had waited nearly an hour when the door opened and Saqr came in, sat back against the cushions next to him, and offered him some sunflower seeds, avoiding any conversation that might lead to me, the skinny sacrificial bride.

A half hour later I went upstairs to them, like the dead rising from the grave, the body wasted away in the soil. Badriya had bought me a white chiffon outfit, the closest thing possible to a wedding dress, given the glaring absence of all signs of a wedding. The guests mumbled in disbelief because I came in alone, without any procession or ululations, carrying the heavy suitcase of my clothing, until Chandra rushed to take it from me. I looked around for the man who'd become my husband.

Badriya hugged me as she took my hand to lead me to the salon to see the groom. I wasn't thinking about Faris, I was thinking about Saqr, about what he'd say had he seen me in a gauzy chiffon dress. My body felt hot. The women started their ululations, and Badriya joined them. Wadha averted her eyes and just walked at the end of the procession. At the door of the salon, Badriya pushed me inside. I didn't look at Faris, and Saqr didn't look at me. Congratulations. He said it while staring at the carpet.

Those are the details of my wedding day, with its suspicious calm and funerary silence. I climbed into the limousine next to Faris. Our hands accidentally brushed against each other and I pulled mine away, drawing it up inside my sleeve. He looked at me, baffled; I averted my eyes. To the Hilton, he said to the driver. He looked at me the whole way, at my painted fingernails hiding inside the sleeves of this disaster.

We entered the hotel suite. It was very beautiful. The couches wrapped around the corner of the room, beige with brown, red, and olive cushions. The bedspread was white cotton like a drifting cloud. There was a twenty-two-inch television and a shiny black kitchenette. The windows went on forever. I felt dizzy. I pulled all the curtains closed and turned to Faris, who was sitting on the edge of the double bed, examining me in great confusion and fighting to overcome his feelings of cowardice. He got control of himself and gave me a little smile. I saw in that smile that he was handsome. I should have smiled back.

"Are you hungry?"

"No."

"I made us dinner reservations."

"I'm a little under the weather."

"Oh?"

I hesitated, then said, "I have my period."

His face reddened and he answered politely: "I hope you feel better. There's no need to go out. We'll eat in the suite."

He lifted the phone to order dinner. I was in the bathroom, pondering—in great disbelief—the size of the Jacuzzi, after seven years of showering standing up. I locked the bathroom door and sat on the cold marble edge. The mirror in front of me was smiling. You devil, Fatima! You like the Jacuzzi more than your husband outside. I laughed, sliding my hand across the white polished surface of this perfectly beautiful thing that I would soon sink into. I turned on the faucet. A waterfall of hot water rushed out and the room filled with steam and the scent of lavender. I emptied all the bottles of soap into the tub and made many bubbles. I soaked there for an hour. For an hour I played, for an hour I was the child I used to be.

When I came out of the bathroom, drying my hair with a towel, Faris was sitting on the couch in front of the television looking for a movie to watch. When he saw me and my ridiculous pajamas he forced a smile and looked at the ground. He'd gotten the message.

"Dinner is cold!" he scolded me gently, pointing at the dinner table with its covered metal trays. I sat on the chair opposite and ate some french fries. I looked at the lasagna, but didn't dare eat it. The presence of this man who'd become my husband made me anxious. I barely ate, and he barely ate. Neither of us were happy with the other. Silence prevailed.

I thanked him and went to the bathroom to brush my teeth. When I came out I found that he'd pushed the long couch closer to the television and spread some pillows out on it. Come here, next to me. We'll watch a movie for a little while then we'll sleep. As he spoke, he patted the spot next to him on the couch.

"I'm tired. I'll go to bed," I said as I buried myself under the comforter. I wrapped the comforter around me for more protection. I smothered my body, shuttered my pores, and disappeared far into myself, an earthworm.

"Are you cold?" Faris asked.

"There's another blanket in the closet," I said. "Good night."

Silence.

"Good night," came his response.

Evening of the Third Day

His hand was wrapped tightly around my neck, nearly breaking it. He stood behind me, an impossible wall, bringing me down to the basement.

The funeral had ended and the crowd dispersed. I said goodbye to my uncle's house and moved with him "far away to here," descending down into the lowest depths of reality. Fourteen steps was all that separated me from the world.

My heart lurched with every step down, seeing the damp blotches spreading across the wall's surface, the green mold peering at me menacingly from the cracks. It was pitch dark and the smell betrayed the slow decay of a place that had died long ago and was decomposing at its leisure. Saqr pressed some switches and the blue lights of the long neon bulbs trembled. There were wires fixed to the wall with tape. The place looked like it had vomited its guts out. The vast desert of what he called my room spread before me, and he gently pushed my shoulder into it, a mouth that opened to swallow me up.

"You'll live with us from now on," he said. "You can be my daughter instead of my sister. You're too young to be my sister anyway. You can be a sister to my children."

My heart filled with anguish and I closed my eyes. This basement is my room? I'm afraid of basements. We have no choice, he'd said. They didn't have any extra rooms. There was a spare room on the second floor but he had decided to fill it with sports equipment.

I looked around. The carpet was dark olive; walking on it scratched the soul. On the ceiling above my head, yellow stains spread out over a white wasteland. The air conditioner droned incessantly. He turned it off and five minutes later the room smelt musty. Since it was a basement, there were no windows. The room looked out only onto its own ugliness, and knew nothing of the world other than the musings that sprouted from its dark woods. The air was heavy with the smell of the little white mothballs scattered here and there. This meant I wasn't alone. I'd entered a utopia of rodents; generations upon generations of cockroaches and mice had established countless civilizations here before I came, with the rapping of my sandals and spasms of fear, crowding in to fight for space.

I would spend seven years of my life in this place. Compared to my pink room at my parents' house, this basement was a cowshed. I cried for days, hugging a picture of my parents. I wept not just over their death but over the death of the carpet in my room, my little chandelier, the floral wallpaper, of how the room smelled of strawberries, many things. I didn't know why, having suddenly lost my parents, I had to lose these things too.

"Where are my things?"

"We got rid of some of them," he said, nodding toward the small pile that remained. Most of them, he meant. I didn't ask why; I was still afraid of his big belly and red skin. But he was generous enough to explain. He went into great detail, telling me why it is forbidden to buy dolls, because they are images of man that keep the angels away, especially "depraved Barbie" that plants debauched ideas in girls' minds. Two new concepts entered into my vocabulary: depravity and debauchery.

With the exception of my bedspread and clothes, I wasn't allowed to hold on to my life. All of the beautiful things departed at once: my mother, my father, my toys and my room, my teddy bear and my big wooden dollhouse. Everything died; everything except me. I was now an orphan, and a pit opened up around me ready to drink from my soul. He said, "Don't worry, you'll get used to the place," and put his hand on my shoulder. His hand was heavy, like the emptiness pulling me under.

The Picture

No, I am not okay.

I spoke to the picture of my mother and father that he'd pulled from its frame. The wrinkled picture, yellowing, twenty years older than me, was taken on the night of my parents' wedding. They were in the large courtyard at my grandfather's house, standing under the branches of a date palm covered in tiny white lights: a time that seemed simple and carefree.

In the picture every inch of my father's body was smiling. He had snagged himself a beautiful wife, twenty-two years his junior, appropriately vivacious, young, innocent, and fit to be a wife for an entire lifetime, after his first wife had died and left him with two sons he didn't know how to raise, because raising children was, as he believed, "women's work." The iqal he wore on his head was slightly crooked, but who would notice that, with all this joy on his face? My mother had braided her hair and decorated it with a string of pearls. She'd told me many times that they were natural pearls. Each one was unique and had its own constrictions and creases. She'd tell me you could only get a necklace like this in Bahrain, where she was from. Like a crazy mermaid, she had decided to go off and marry a widower as a kind of adventure. "If you get married," she'd said to me once when I was looking at their wedding pictures, "we'll fix your hair the same way." I was lying on their double bed, my legs dancing excitedly. "Then you'll do the same thing for your daughter and it will become a family tradition."

How would my mother feel if she knew how I got married, without anyone paying attention, as if they were covering up a scandal? And if she knew that I was hopelessly infertile, that I wouldn't have a daughter or a son, or anything remotely like one.

In another picture, a different one, two other faces appear: Saqr and Fahd, my half brothers. Saqr is fourteen, round, a smile on his face, a frown in his eyes. Fahd, skinny and sad, is ten. He died from a fever four months after his father remarried.

My father's late wife lost all the girls and gave birth to two boys before dying of kidney failure. Her story ends there so another story can begin. How could an eighteen-year-old girl raise that somber boy just four years younger than her? I don't know how she did it.

When I was born my mother was twenty. Saqr was sixteen. By the time I was two years old, he had gone away to school. He came back a year later with a long beard and wearing a shortened thawb, the number eleven still in place between his eyebrows. My father had to pay the costs the state had incurred to send him away for the year. Saqr settled for a vocational training certificate and went to work as an official in the Ministry of Interior's archives, another faraway basement holding thousands of files.

When he was twenty-one, Saqr decided to get married. I was five. I don't remember anything about the days Saqr and I lived together under the same roof. He married Badriya and had Wadha, who is three years younger than me. His wife continued having children, more and more children, because he asked for them. There was always room for another child to whom he would provide a proper upbringing for the betterment of the ummah—the Islamic community. That was the whole point.

That story is in another photograph. But this one that concerns me, it's just of my father and my mother. My middle-aged father whose eyes overflow with happiness, and my mother, who barely looks at the camera, barely smiles, in her dress with the long lace sleeves and pearl buttons, a bouquet of jasmine in her hands.

They must have been good together. I think about that now as I contemplate my marriage that is about to end. No doubt theirs was an exceptional marriage, in order to deserve this end, to die together, in a car accident on Arar Road, after returning from Jordan where they'd closed a deal to buy seven pieces of land for no more than 1,700 dinars each. The deal of a lifetime! my father, who could smell a good deal a million miles away, had said. He closed the deal of a lifetime and reached the end of his own.

The Republic of the Big Brother

HE WAS MY HALF BROTHER but I was an orphan, alone. For Saqr, me becoming an orphan was a gift sent from heaven. He could now be responsible for me. I could be his project; he would reform me, set me straight.

Even before he knew me he was convinced that I was disturbed, or at best broken and in need of repair. He'd had his differences with my parents and disapproved of many things that they did: listening to music, buying Barbies, displaying photographs on tables for decoration, celebrating birthdays, going to weddings in hotels. With me, Saqr was pursuing a noble mission called "save what is possible to save."

I was the victim of too much love, of following passion and losing one's inner compass. Saqr believed he had to save me from my misguided ways, now that it was in his power, now that he alone held the power of being my sole guardian. Now he would have his revenge on me, his thirteen-year-old half sister, for being his half sister.

He came to my room all the time. I was the daughter whose waywardness he had resolved to correct, as if I were a prisoner, as if he were a warden. He put me under a microscope to make sure things were running well on this mythical bridge where he was working to rehabilitate me so I'd be worthy of his paradise: Barbie no longer pollutes my head with debauched thoughts, I took the photos of my parents off the night table so as not to chase the angels away, I don't draw butterflies on my notebook, I don't read Bibliothèque verte books that fill my head with harmful stories about laughing swans, people turning into birds, and charming genies that emerge from lemons—stories he called "nonsense."

I don't chew gum in public. I only sit in the family sections of restaurants. I don't wear pants. I don't listen to music. I don't watch movies. I don't buy books that aren't "beneficial." I don't sit alone. I don't go to the hairdresser. I only visit certain homes. Everything was prohibited, with few exceptions.

He was stuffing me full of reality, the reality of being an orphan, of being alone, and the arid life that he had chosen for me. Every time he plucked another feather from my heart and stole one of my many skies, he would remind me that the world is a prison for the believer and heaven for the disbeliever, and that holding fast to one's religion is like holding on to a hot coal.

I was a girl on the verge of puberty, about to become a woman. Therefore, he—the older brother ruling my life like a curse—was to prepare me for my heavenly and sacred role in this world: to make of me a sound wife, devoted and fecund, who would have more and more children, girls who would start wearing the hijab at age four and follow me around like dyed chicks, and boys who would go to the "Buds of Light" and "Guiding Light" camps, where they'd dwell on the fall of al-Andalus and head out on imaginary conquests, awaiting that moment—that would be a disaster for the whole world—when they would be the ones in power and could devote themselves to destroying everything.

Everything had already been decided for me. All I had to do was to follow the proper guidelines in order to do things the right way—simple practical steps that didn't require a lot of thought. Actually, they required one not to think at all, and one's skill at this was linked to how capable one was of not thinking.

In order to be worthy of this sacred duty of mine, I had a lot to learn. I had to read endless booklets—*The Horrors of*

Judgment Day, Torments of the Grave, 1000 Questions and Answers for Women, and so on. These were the only things suitable for me to read. There was also a long list of tapes full of preaching, hollering, and crying to treat my mental illness.

For the first week after the accident, when the features of my new life as an orphan were revealed and opened up like a wound, I buried myself under the bedspread and wept, wondering if the unbelievable horror of my life was just a dream. I pinched myself and slapped my face. I couldn't shake the nightmare.

On one of his rounds he found me crying under the pillows. Are you crying, Fatima? Your mother and father don't need your tears, they need your prayers. He talked for a whole hour about how the believer must submit to fate and how the dead are tortured by the cries of their family, and told me that every tear I shed held dire consequences for my parents in their afterlife. Each word turned the tears in my eyes to stone; each tear was a burning hot coal.

He spoke robotically—all he had to do was open his mouth and the words poured out, neatly ordered and arranged. Each word knew its place, as if they had been waiting inside him the whole time, as if they had grown tired of waiting, as if they could not believe he opened his mouth to summon them, until they appeared there, floating in the air, like a green genie.

That was the first religious lecture that Saqr gave me, for the sake of bringing me up right, when he could have just given me a hug.

My Wedding Dress

THE NEXT MORNING I OPENED my eyes to the curtains in the hotel bedroom. They were a soft cream color, framing the window. Beautiful curtains, porous and enigmatic, curtains of fine lace, impossibly feminine. They were the first thing I saw that morning, the morning I became a married woman, still a virgin, wound up in the comforter like a caterpillar.

The lace curtains said good morning. Good morning! I said. Good morning, lace curtains. You're very beautiful! Did you sleep well? Yes, thank you. I slept well—this bed is incredible! I am happy to hear that. Thank you, dear curtains . . . We exchanged courtesies, then fell silent, the lace curtains and I. I looked at them, they looked at me. I touched them, reached my hand out to examine the immensely beautiful lace, perfect in itself, whose designs were endlessly suggestive. This fabric was so lovely. So lovely!

I decided that these curtains would be my wedding dress.

Then I grew aware of the deep sound of his breathing. I looked behind me and saw him, sleeping like a child. He was handsome, with beautifully arched eyebrows and thick eyelashes, a lovely tan complexion, prominent cheekbones, dark lips. I wondered if he smoked. He had broad shoulders, a wide chest. Tall and slender. He was ideal, this knight, Faris, except that he'd never once been a part of any of my dreams.

*

I liked him and feared him. I couldn't believe how real he looked. Did I really marry this man? Who is he? A minute later I had one thought in my head.

I have to get out of here.

Starving at the Dinner Table

IT HAPPENED EVERY DAY AT the dinner table. Everyone would get their daily dose of praise and adulation and leave feeling happy. Everyone except me.

It always began the same way. Saqr would ask his children what they did that day. They would rush to answer, launching into a performance they'd rehearsed many times. The Arabic teacher liked my essay. They selected me to be on the show about Kuwaiti students. Ms. Wafaa praised my recitation. Convening these sessions was the perfect way for Saqr to convince the members of his family that they were better than others, that God had favored them over His other creations by granting them the privilege of belonging to this holy house. His house. God's chosen house.

I followed the conversation from the deepest of the wounds I'd acquired after my parents died. I could feel their hands reaching deep inside me and pulling the scabs off, could feel the pus oozing out, listening to this dialogue between the proud father and his even prouder children, everyone bragging about the other and repeating their virtues. Every atom of my body wanted to walk onstage and join the scene, to enter the blessed spotlight of love and acceptance. I found myself listening through one of the holes in my loneliness to the conversations at the table, my eyes as wide as the disaster itself, my heart starving.

With time I started to feign deafness. I got so good at pretending that I eventually grew deaf. The voices coming

37

out of their mouths turned into a kind of hum. The world hummed while I chewed. I now knew people could blot out their senses if they wanted to. This brought me a kind of relief. Deafness swallowed me up and the more it did the deeper I sank into a gauzy haze. Years later I learned that this blue fog was poetry.

One time I tried to play along. I'd gotten a good grade on a math test after doing poorly at school in the months following the accident, and I brought the test with me. I folded the paper and hid it in my pocket, hungrily anticipating the moment Saqr would glance my way. He didn't. When he had nothing else to say he belched and shook his hands so bits of rice flew across the table.

"Thanks be to God," he said, standing up and wiping his tongue across his teeth.

The only thing Saqr was interested in when it came to me was the discovery of a new flaw. He hadn't looked at me the entire time.

"Saqr?"

"Yes."

I took the paper out of my pocket and slid it over it to him. Seventeen and a half out of twenty. My parents died nine months ago and this was the best grade I'd gotten since the car rolled over and the world turned upside down. Here I am, Saqr, filled with despair and knocking at the doors of your happy paradise. Say something nice to me to keep me going, before the ugliness takes over completely.

"What's this?"

"A math test."

"You got seventeen and a half out of twenty?"

"Yes."

"Ooof. Why?"

My body was paralyzed from the force of the surprise. A laugh escaped from Wadha's mouth.

"Shame on you!" whispered Badriya.

38

Saqr put his hand on my shoulder. "Work harder next time."

I struggled to open my mouth. "Seventeen and a half out of twenty isn't good?"

"No, it's not good."

"Why isn't it good?"

He asked his children, "What do you think, is seventeen and a half out of twenty good?"

"Not good!"

"Why not?"

They raised their hands like they were in a classroom. Me! Me! Me! They fought with each other to answer. Their answers were unexpected:

"The ummah needs children who are hardworking!"

"There's a hadith that says God is pleased with those who, when they do something, do it well."

Great words. Fine words. But I just wanted to hear something nice. The praise I was seeking turned into a condemnation. I folded the paper over and over in my hand, folded it until it disappeared.

After that I didn't try too hard to give Saqr reasons to like me. Things got worse at school. I stood in the back of the classroom throughout math class because I forgot the multiplication table for the number six. The religion teacher hit the palm of my hand with a ruler because I forgot my hijab. Each day school turned into another tomb.

When I received a report card covered in inverted flags after the quarterly assessment, I forged his signature so he wouldn't find out about my poor grades. I returned the report card to my teacher the next day thinking that I had saved myself a public shaming. Two hours later the vice principal was standing at the door of the classroom and asking for the students whose names were written on a scrap of yellow paper. My name was on that paper, the paper of shame.

We were led like a flock of sheep, trembling in fear. She led us to her office and started shouting in our faces until we burst into tears. No one could hold out against Mrs. Ghunay-ma's face screaming just four fingers away from our noses. She informed us that she had called our families and told them of the matter, and that anyone who did it again would be sus-pended from school for three days.

I went home, wondering what Saqr would do. It was no longer just about my poor grades; it was also about forging his personal signature.

I anticipated a harsh rebuke, sitting down to a meal of obscene language and invective at the dinner table. Come, let's criticize Fatima's failure at school. Come, let's attack Fati-ma's morals, Fatima who lies and forges signatures. Come, let her be a lesson to you. Fatima, the being cut into and under-going reformation.

What happened was worse.

When I joined them for lunch, he looked at me neutrally then burst into laughter. A vengeful phosphoric glimmer shone in his eyes; almost an hour went by with him and his family laughing at me. You see how you messed up? Why don't you study? He laughed and they laughed, while I tried to smile and tried not to cry. Tried to laugh at myself with them and failed.

After that incident, my brother, impelled by his good intentions to guide me onto the path of serious work, made a subtle change to my name. Having been "Fatima," I became "Fashila." Failure.

Yes, yes, I know.

He did it to motivate me, that's all.

Tom and Jerry

I COULD NO LONGER PRETEND to be asleep nor lull myself back to sleep after that night that I spent, my back turned to my groom, wrapped up in all of the covers, curled up like a snail. It was after seven in the morning. I could no longer resist the idea that had, with its uncontrollable lust, taken control of every cell of my body.

The man who was now my husband was very much asleep. The television was very much on, and the remote control was very much lying on the couch in front of me, saying, Come, Fatima. Touch me. Feel my keys. See my potential. Come, dear, love me as one should, I promise you horizons and music. I will give you the world, Fatima. Come love me!

The temptation was manifold. I found myself gently pulling my body from the covers and going to the couch to change the channel. I felt that I held in my hand an unvanquishable power, as if I could go to thousands of cities while sitting in my hotel room in my pajamas that smiled and winked.

I changed the channels, staring at the screen, mouth agape. The wonder I felt made me sad. I was looking for films, none of which I'd seen for years, but to my surprise I found myself frozen in front of the cartoons, watching with hungry eyes and feeling myself coming back, young and fresh and new.

For a moment I imagined that I was fine. My mother was in the kitchen frying eggs and my father would be home in a few minutes. I, a young girl with a long braid, inhaled the scent of my childhood, a small spot of chocolate milk on the collar of my pink pajamas.

The morning after our wedding night, I was awake, alone, remote control in hand. I felt I'd been given the rarest of red camels and was ready to make up for long years of life spent outside of life. That was all that mattered then.

Not marriage, not the man sleeping in my bed without a blanket, not the oppressive turn my life had taken. Nothing mattered now but Tom and Jerry.

A Ripe Banana

Friday morning Saqr asked me to put on my abaya to accompany him to prayers. I mentioned that he'd told me it was better for a woman to pray at home. He said this was for my own good because I had become like a "ripe banana" no one wanted to eat, and he had to do something about it.

I was seventeen years old when Saqr informed me in his special way that I was an old maid: I was a ripe banana and no one would want to eat me.

His plan was simply for one of his friends to see me and wish to have me. Of course I would be most suitable as a second or third wife, assuming his friends were his age. When the prayer ended and the crowd dispersed, I was the only one left in the women's prayer area. I sat on the red carpet that had been spread out. O Almighty, make me invisible. Make me disappear.

I stayed in the women's prayer area waiting for the time to pass, for everyone to leave, and for Saqr to boil under the sun, trying to delay those of his friends he believed would be suitable as a brother-in-law. He was doing what he could, and I was doing what I could. An hour went by until everyone had left. One remained.

"Hey! Hey boy!" Saqr had lost his patience and started calling out to me. Naturally, he was calling me "boy" so as not to cause a scandal by saying my name within earshot of a strange man, even if this strange man had been promised a chance to devour me with his profoundly ravenous eyes moments later. He'd told one of his acquaintances about me. My sister, I raised her myself, she wants to settle down and get married! The man Saqr happened to choose—randomly and most likely due to fleeting circumstance more than anything else—was between forty and forty-five years old, skinny, with a hennaed beard, a crooked nose, and a shaved moustache. Saqr repeated, "Boy! Come out, boy!" Then he risked poking his head inside the women's prayer area. He spotted the corner of my abaya and knew I was hiding next to the entrance. My heart was pounding. When he knew I was alone inside he took a few steps in and pulled me by my hijab.

"What are you doing? I've been calling you for an hour with no reply!"

"I'm praying! Praying!"

"Right. The tarawih, you realize, are performed in Ramadan. Get moving."

He pushed me before his friend, joking with him and repeating, "She's being bashful! I raised my sister myself. I raised her to have good manners and avert her gaze." I felt the man's glances piercing my face and injuring my spirit, as if I were a car, new shoes, or maybe, in this case, a race camel being traded.

I hurried to the car and sat in the back seat holding back my tears.

We arrived home. I ran to the kitchen with Saqr chasing and threatening me. I picked up a kitchen knife and put it to my cheek. "I'll do it!" I said. "By God, I'll do it! I'll slice my face and throw the pieces at your feet if you force me to get married. Then no one will want to marry me ever."

"You're crazy! You foolish girl! I want the best for you! I chose the best for you!"

"You can keep him. I don't want him!"

"Abu Fahd has lots and lots of money. You won't have to work or even finish school. He will give you a comfortable life!"

"I don't want him! I don't want him! I'd rather have a hard life."

"It's true, you lack intellect."

He said it stressing his pronunciation syllable by syllable. He pulled the letters out carefully, picking them from his teeth: You lack intellect. He was referencing a hadith, and naturally he also said, "And religion."

A Lone Sheep

SAQR IS THE OLDER BROTHER and guardian. The guardian must be obeyed.

The guardian's decisions are always correct because the guardian is the one most capable of discerning and securing my interests. Any disagreement with the guardian is the devil's work. The guardian loves me, wants what is best for me, and does not guide me except in the way of right conduct. The guardian leads me only onto the wise path. The guardian makes all of my decisions on my behalf, from my clothing to my choice of friends, because he—given his experience and superiority—knows what is best for me better than I do. There is no need to ever think about the guardian's existence because he—with his superior intellect—has spared me the trouble of thinking and making my own decisions. Everything has been settled, life is a recipe that has been written out step by step, and all I have to do is follow the right procedure to obtain the desired result—the meal that is me.

Saqr treated his status as my guardian as pure fate. If God Almighty was the one who decided, when he planned the accident and foreordained my parents' death, to place me in Saqr's care, then Saqr was performing a divine role in raising me. He became an expert in my affairs, as if I were his latest hobby.

He took the accident well, and spoke about it as if it didn't concern him. He could repeat the gruesome details and explain how the car rolled over four times, landing "like a beetle flipped on its back"—that was the expression he used—and that the coroner said the deaths had occurred quickly. Then Saqr would say that the property they had gone to buy in Amman was a good decision and still generating profit. After that, he'd ask for God's mercy and forgiveness for them.

The way he dealt with their death was unbearably superficial. I would have preferred to be silent a thousand years than talk about their death this way. I ended up withdrawing from their gatherings and hiding in my basement, which had started to resemble me and the fissures in my spirit, from the yellow blotches on the ceiling to the cracks in the wall.

Solitude wasn't an easy choice. It was considered the work of the devil in my older brother's house. The family gatherings occurred through pressure and asserting the necessity of obedience and involvement in the group, because the absence of my desire to sit with my older brother, my guardian and benefactor, was something that made it easier for the devil to influence those of us who are far off by themselves, the "lone sheep" as he called us.

Once I asked him how to understand the Prophet's desire for seclusion in the Cave of Hira. He laughed and his stomach jiggled to the left and right as if he'd swallowed a sea. "You think you can compare yourself to the Prophet Muhammad?"

Any relation I had to the sacred, to God, to the Prophet, and to the Quran had to go through him, because I was branded with ignorance and inferiority. I, with my questions and my solitude, emboldened myself against that invisible priesthood that was choking my world. I was dizzy with questions, pained by them. They were all forbidden and sealed with red wax: boxes of taboos that were not to be touched and that no one had the right to discuss. For the world, as Saqr believed, was merely a series of interconnected channels. All we had to do was pass the truth that we already possessed to those below us, and to receive it from those above us. We don't need to search for it, because we were born lucky, we who know and don't need to figure things out for ourselves. All such efforts lead nowhere; there is no excuse for my wasted effort. It is heresy, a lack of faith. Every question is abhorrent. Every question is an atheist scheme.

So much did religiosity dominate my world that religion seemed to be something unattainable. In the end, I wasn't allowed to be me. The bulk of Saqr's lectures served his efforts to break me. To wipe out those things that so annoyed him, the things that made me different. I was a lone sheep, a ripe banana, and inferior no matter what.

Solitude wasn't a given. I had to fight for it, to draw out its features in a dotted red line, asserting, yes, it's ugly, but it's my tomb, it's my place, it's where I can be. The alarm inside me would wail in panic whenever I heard Saqr's sandals slapping the steps, coming down to me. I was always forced to make excuses for the things I did, whether I was doing nothing or paging through *Cinderella*.

I was tired of being me—not allowed to be me and not allowed to be anyone but me. I was tired and worn out and wasted but I didn't have the luxury of feeling tired, as I had to fight to hold on to the few choices that remained mine. To fight for myself, me. Who am I? This thing that they were trying to break and destroy and bury alive, this dangerous thing that, it seemed, threatened to take down the whole system by merely reading a novel? Yes, that.

I am trying to capture seven years of prison life in as few words as possible, and thus with as little emotion as possible. I repeat to myself that I have to write everything in that cold, lofty language of the newspapers. I want to forget that I was the child whose name was in the news, who was raped of her childhood.

There is something not understood about the shame victims feel for being victims. There is always that mean voice deep inside that says: I shouldn't have made a mistake, I shouldn't have been a victim.

Why are victims ashamed of the chains around their wrists?

The Black Screen on the White Horse

IN THE BEGINNING I WASN'T Faris's wife as much as I was the wife of the twenty-two-inch plasma screen, radiant of brow, broad shouldered, smooth to the touch, with its shiny black frame—the screen of my dreams! The black screen on the white horse, more handsome than all the men in the world, magnificent as a magic crystal, brimming with thousands of worlds capable of smuggling me out of my reality, immersing me in images, and images of images, granting to me many and varied lives, without basements or ghosts or the slapping of sandals on my thigh or hands forcing food into my mouth. As if life hadn't boarded its train and left.

In the days following my wedding, I felt the blood rush to my head, hot and excited, as I stood where the great explorers stood, to discover—with tremendous confusion and an open mouth—a satellite channel called MBC2, just for films, that showed movies around the clock, like an impossible grandmother who doesn't die.

"This channel only shows movies?" I asked Faris, who was fidgety and restless from my refusal to leave the suite all morning.

"MBC2?" he said derisively.

"Yes."

"You've never heard of this channel?"

"How can they show films twenty-four hours a day?"

"What's so strange about that?"

"Are there that many films in the world that they can show them constantly, seven days a week, thirty days a month, three hundred and sixty-five days a year?"

Faris laughed.

I wasn't hurt. I just wanted answers. I asked again: "How long have people been making films?"

"I don't know! Since Charlie Chaplin?"

"Who?"

"How could you not know about this channel?"

"Oh well, you know, things like this happen."

Yes. They do.

People become orphans. Childhoods are kidnapped. You can be imprisoned in a basement, kept out of school, your love for life can be stolen, your books burned, your poems drowned in a bucketful of tears. You can be dragged outside your poem, hands pulling you by the hair, wetting yourself from the fear. Anything can happen, except for a satellite channel that shows films around the clock.

"The television in our house was encrypted."

I said it as an explanation, not an apology, then turned away from him to continue watching the movie with my full attention. Television, my master, my first husband. I keep him turned on all the time, even when I leave the room, even when sleeping or while reading. The background noise tells me I am no longer in the basement.

Throughout our marriage Faris complained, Is the television in this house ever off?

No, it isn't. If I turn it off, the fear will reach me, the silence will descend, and the loneliness will gobble me up. The ghosts will return, the poisoned apple, the devils that nest in the dark mirrors. The cockroaches will come back, and the rats, and the many hands that fall from the heights of their tyranny onto my body. If I turn off the television everything will disappear and I will return—a time traveler—to that hell set aside just for me. I will feel I am there, hurled into the filthy hell that came when I lost my mother and father, in the basement tomb. If we sat at the dinner table and the television was off, I'd get up and turn it on. If we wanted to go to bed and the television was off, I'd get up and turn it on. If we wanted to go out and the television was off, I'd turn it on before locking the apartment door twice with the key, so the place wouldn't fill with the demons of the past. I will always turn it on, all the time. If possible, I wanted to be buried with it, just like the pharaohs.

Eclipse

THE YEAR OF THE ACCIDENT was the year I started wearing the hijab.

I thought Saqr would love me more if I did it. He praised Wadha whenever we went out on weekends, pointing at her face that was "as lovely as a full moon," lit "by a divine light" cast down on it from God's heavens and reflecting the heart of a woman filled with faith. I wanted some of that light. For heaven to look at me, for beautiful things to happen to me for a change.

So I decided—in an attempt to gain my older brother's acceptance—to start wearing the hijab, to become part of this group, to do what I had to do to get my share of affection.

I put on the hijab and no one told me I looked as lovely as the moon, that the light of faith radiated from my pretty brow, that my eyes sparkled in a new way. They didn't have a party for me and didn't give me any gifts. Badriya bought me over-sized tunics and full-length skirts from Marks and Spencer, a white veil made of crepe and another of cotton. "Congratulations, dear," she said, patting my shoulder as Saqr chewed on his miswak and mumbled, "Good! Good! Next you'll start wearing the niqab, God willing." Wadha said that I'd started to look like an Afghani refugee.

The festivities ended quickly and the gathering dispersed. I didn't hear the word 'moon' or the word 'light' or the word 'faith.' And I didn't understand what mistake I'd made this time that had caused things to go poorly. During that period, when I was still partly a child and not quite a woman, I thought everything was my fault, and that my unerring brother was firmly protected by the sacred.

Saqr left. Badriya disappeared into the kitchen. Wadha went up to her bedroom and the younger kids continued running around. Why had the party ended quickly? Where were the sweets, where were the hugs and congratulations?

I returned to my basement, which had slowly started turning into a tortoise shell. I took the picture of my mother and father out of the drawer and looked into my mother's pale face, at the part in her hair and the pearls she was wearing, the lace sleeves. I'm becoming a woman, Mama. It's not as fun as I thought it would be. It's not good to be a woman, in this place at least. Maybe if I was going to be another woman, not the one I'm supposed to be when I grow up, maybe then it would have been very nice. Mama, I wish I hadn't been born.

The Fog

"FATIMA? FATIMA . . . ? WHAT'S WRONG?"

The blue fog dissipated. I had a mist in my eyes and a poem in my heart. The things around me started to appear clothed in their material existence and sank under the weight. Their edges, colors, forms, and dimensions appeared; music spread through the air. I looked around me and took in the place. The spaces of this restaurant in Thailand were wrapped in a lavish green. There were wooden masks on the wall and an old wooden bridge that ran over a pond of golden fish with puffy cheeks swallowing bubbles to an island of wooden cabanas, each with about four tables, orchids, and a sea extending outside the window. The place was too beautiful.

"What's wrong?"

"What happened?"

"Did you hear anything I said?"

"What did you say?"

"You're kidding. Have I been talking to myself for an hour?"

"I'm sorry."

I put down my fork. I folded my fingers into a fist and they curled up inside the palm of my hand. I left the cup of jasmine tea on the table and looked at it. I must not disappear.

How can I explain to him? How can I explain that I become deaf when I sit at a dinner table, that for seven years it was my way of saving myself from the hunger tearing at my insides?

How can I explain that I dive into a bottomless absence, in the eternal blue fog, between many clouds and black holes. It was pointless to explain to the man who had become my husband just yesterday that I was in this much pain.

"What were you saying?"

I decided to stop eating, in order to prevent myself from wandering off into the twilight that spread through my chest.

"I was saying that the marriage happened quickly."

"Yes."

"We didn't have a chance to get to know each other."

"It's the tradition of both families."

"I respect tradition."

"Really?"

"Yes, it makes things run more smoothly."

"I don't respect it."

He looked surprised. "What do you mean?"

"I mean that we are burdened by enough cages. If we'd met before getting married, for example, many things might have been revealed to both of us about the other. You know, something better than this scratch-and-win marriage."

He smiled. "Well, I won, at least."

"Are you kidding?"

"Why would I be kidding? I have a beautiful bride."

I laughed. I no longer heard this word in my life. I'd read it once, in a letter, in another story, in a wayward beat, in a poem.

"Fatima? Fatima . . . ? Fatima!"

"Oh . . . sorry."

"Where were you?"

"I—I don't know."

"Did you hear what I said?"

"No."

"I said, tell me about yourself, so I can know you."

"Socrates."

"I'm sorry?"

"Socrates said that."

"Socrates said what?"

"Speak so I can see you."

I smiled. He almost shouted, surprised: "You're educated!"

"Because I know a famous quote by Socrates?"

"It's not nothing."

"I know Socrates and I don't know MBC2. That means nothing."

He burst out laughing and clapped his hands while shaking his head. I didn't know I was funny.

My Birthday Present

ON THE DAY OF MY twentieth birthday, which no one remembered, or which everyone remembered but pretended to forget because "birthdays are haram," I felt like I owed it to myself to try.

"What were you trying to do, Fatima?"

"I was trying to live."

I said to myself: If there's someone in this world who can help me, I'm going to knock on their door. Unfortunately, this brilliant idea didn't come to me until after nine in the evening. I put on my hijab and my shabby old abaya and went out. Saqr asked me where I was going. To the bookstore—I forgot to buy something important for tomorrow's class. He told me not to be late.

I went to Jabriya and walked slowly by the many clinics. I was certain that I'd seen a mental health clinic here. Maybe that's what I needed to get rid of the problem, I thought. What was the problem? I wasn't sure. Maybe the problem was that I was me, and that the world was the world, and that we—the world and I—weren't getting along as we should, and needed to come to terms with some things.

I went to the clinic, without pausing for a moment. In fact, I was going over the lines I had decided to recite to the doctor: Doctor! I am completely broken and I need to be saved. Give me something to help me adjust to the world.

I imagined that he would laugh, but I had nothing to lose, with all the tears that had started flowing so liberally, thinking sardonically about the fact that I was giving myself a trip to a psychologist for my twentieth birthday.

The clinic was closed, and I was enraged. Even though I knew there were security cameras, I started kicking the door. I kicked the door three times and left.

I didn't go back. I didn't go back because for the days that followed I imagined the doctor and the security guard watching the recording of a broken girl kicking the door. Perhaps the security guard was laughing with the doctor and asking him, No offense, Doc, but is this one of the crazies that comes to see you?

The Amusement Park

GOING WITH THEM TO THE amusement park was a mistake.

Maybe I shouldn't have screamed. But the way the ride took off, high in the sky, piercing through the air and hurling me up, the blood rushing in my head hot and fast—it seemed the ride was designed solely to provide an excuse to scream in the world's face. And I screamed, out of fear, and out of pleasure too.

I used to scream, before my parents died, and my mother would shout with me while my father held a camera in his right hand and waved at us. Now the rules have changed. What was halal is now haram, what was allowed is now discouraged, and what was beautiful has become ugly. Excitement is no longer a good thing; indulging in anticipation that causes the breath to catch is no longer acceptable. Now I understand—I understand that I should have done everything silently, under layer after layer of unfeeling. Numbness, then, is the real feminine virtue.

The scream that escaped me, when the ride was taking me up, up, and up, higher and higher, farther than I could believe, this scream, I had no right to it, it wasn't mine. It belonged to men alone.

Many things were revealed to me on that visit to the amusement park. First, I am not allowed to buy anything red to drink so my lips and tongue don't turn pink, making it seem—God forbid—like I am wearing makeup. Second, riding on horses isn't allowed; riding in carriages is. Third, no running or rushing where men can see you. Fourth, buying ice cream is allowed but it must be eaten in such a manner that my tongue doesn't show. Fifth, excitement must be contained and screaming is not allowed, because screaming is a sign of shamelessness and immodesty.

I was dying of laughter when I got off that ride. The peals of laughter shot back inside me like knives under the force of the profanity he spat in my face: You animal! You idiot! He said it in front of people, in front of everyone. When Saqr gets mad, he forgets his miswak and his beard and starts swearing. Why are you screaming, you animal? Are you trying to get men to pay attention to you? Do I have to hit you over the head with a shoe for you to learn some manners?

Yikes. It was truly a surprise, for my screams to have so many dimensions. I didn't know I was so laden with explosives, explosives that might be set off by one unthinking action on my part. Badriya touched his forearm, telling him to forgive me because I was a child. Wadha was looking at me out of the corners of her eyes, the evil glimmering in them, and the younger kids ran off toward another ride, drinking up existence without reservation.

I had missed out on being a child.

The Rule and the Proof

THE LIGHTS BLIND MY EYES; the expanse is too vast. This world is a sea and I am woozy. The smells crowd my nose and the sounds jumble together. I hear the squeaking wheels of carts and suitcases on the shiny tiles. I see mouths opening and clos- ing, opening and closing, as if there were some sense to it. Where did all this world come from? Why is the air filled with noise, why do voices hover over the place like a hive of bees? Where is the honey? Where is the meaning?

He held onto my wrist, pulling me to the right, the left. Right, left. He held me back from this and pushed me away from that. His arms were wrapped around my body as if he were afraid I'd be crushed underfoot. Come this way. Watch out for the wet floor. Why didn't you latch your suitcase properly? He grumbled, secured it, then kept walking, hold- ing me by my wrist. Hey! Hey! Sir, pay attention. Don't you see her passing by? We move. He looks at his watch. We'll be right on time. A voice echoes and the air is filled with unin- telligible sounds. He says, This is our flight. His eyes shine. Let's hurry! I want to say to him, Slow down, slow down, but I can't. I just got out of the coffin—the light hurts my eyes and the sounds frighten me. I need to get used to the expanse and to being in the world.

Are you excited? He asked me that while we stood in the passport line, while we made our way slowly through the departure hall, while we were about to get on the plane. Why did he ask me so many times? What did I answer? Or did I not answer at all and that was why the poor man kept asking? Does he see the fear of the unknown in my eyes and is waiting for a glimmer of happiness or delight? I nodded, swallowed, and held on to his arm, as if he were the only stable thing in a world rocking mercilessly.

How could I tell him it was too much for me? I didn't. Because the moment I reached my seat on the plane I saw the small television screen affixed to the seat in front of me, and was unable to believe it had followed me here. I smiled at it and it smiled back, saying, It's true, I won't leave you. I felt reassured and my body relaxed into the seat. Faris laughed. Why did he laugh?

"You're just like a child."

"What do you mean?"

"You always have this expression on your face . . ."

He opened his eyes wide, raised his eyebrows, and pursed his lips. Do I really look like that? Apparently I gave him the same look because he shook his head, laughing, with a touch of disbelief. Then he reached behind my back, pulled out the seat belt, and secured it around my waist.

He behaved with a kind of superiority while fastening my seat belt and closing my handbag. As if I were a five-year-old girl. Was I, in fact, a five-year-old girl?

"I take it you haven't traveled much."

"Just when I was young."

"Where?"

"To Egypt. London. Lebanon."

"Then what happened?"

"Nothing happened." After a pause, I added dully, "My parents died and things changed."

"How?"

"Saqr became my guardian and he, well . . . He has a different point of view on these things."

"Doesn't Saqr ever travel?"

"Of course. For the hajj and umrah." I swallowed and added, "Saqr says tourism is forbidden, citing the hadith that says there is no 'siyaha' in Islam."

"I think he misunderstood."

"On the contrary. He never misunderstands. It's a mursal hadith, he checked. And Saqr knows that it's mursal, that Sheikh al-Albani classified it as weak. He also knows that were it true it would have another meaning, a different meaning, and that the word 'siyaha' can't logically mean 'tourism,' because this is a new meaning of an old word. 'Siyaha' used to mean to enter monastic life, to shun earthly work and live on charity. But that doesn't matter; what matters is that he never misunderstands anything. He understood it very well, and memorized all of its various narrations and sources, but he interpreted it the way he likes, the way that keeps him from spending his money. That's all."

He seemed surprised by my words, hesitant, and commented, "It seems there are some misunderstandings between you two."

"Saqr and I? On the contrary, we understand each other very well. We can read each other's innermost thoughts. In fact, I don't think there is anyone who knows Saqr like I do, not even his wife. He and I are something special."

"I'm happy to know that."

Faris smiled anxiously. I didn't smile. Once the desert of silence had spread between us, vast and desolate, he asked me again: "Are you excited?"

Traveling without a Mahram

THE FIRST TIME I TRAVELED without going anywhere, it was through a foreign language.

I was sixteen years old when I first met the French language, in my third year of secondary school. Since I was in the literature division, I was required to explore and touch the world of this language, and to allow it to touch me, in my hidden-away heart. It became something I was passionate about.

A week after registration for classes for the new semester, Saqr spotted the French textbook in my hand while I was getting ready to leave for school. He snatched it from me.

"What's this?" he asked in disbelief.

"A French textbook."

"And why is Your Highness registered for French?"

"What's wrong with that?"

"Are we going to abandon the language of the Quran and spend our whole lives studying the language of the unbelievers?"

"French is required for literature students."

"You're in the literature division?"

"You didn't know?"

"Why don't you study something respectable? Science, math . . ."

"My grades weren't good enough."

"And why not? Because you don't study!"

There wasn't anything for me to say, because I have been branded with suspicion and everything is my fault.

"This is what happens when you mess up."

He said it while opening the book with the tips of his fingers, as if he were touching something contaminated. He paged through it a little, his face sullen, disgusted. I didn't understand the point of paging through a book you couldn't understand. "What a joke. This is a defeated ummah, from head to toe! Uncertain of who we are, infatuated by the West, imitating the unbelievers in everything!"

He said Arabic is the best of all languages, that it's the most beautiful and eloquent language on earth, that it's the language of Paradise, that I should be proud of it instead of studying the "language of unbelievers." I would have liked to ask him: How is learning French an insult to Arabic? How is it possible for there to be a believer language and an unbeliever language? But I didn't dare. I lowered my gaze and started trying to get out of the situation while he went on about his love and passion for Arabic, even though he frequently mispronounced and misspelled words and mercilessly rendered all verbs in the accusative case, right or wrong.

Even though it was a very basic course, I was charmed by the beauty of French. It made me happy that life could be different. A language that is like music—you love the way it feels in your ear and in your mouth, you put its vocabulary in your heart and experience its lightness, its flutter, its coquettishness, and its ability to melt on your tongue. A dancing language, filled with elongations, inflections, and elisions, and many silent letters, like boxes filled with secrets. If you dare to speak it, you feel you're speaking with a tongue full of honey, afraid the honey will spill, that it will drip from the corners of your lips; you worry that the honey will slip out and you'll be left without.

I paged through the book every day to find a new word. I'd spell out its letters, both silent and pronounced. I'd trace it on my palm, hide it in my mouth. I explored this new world like the discoverers going to the ends of the earth: an entire continent of my own. I buried myself under dozens of pillows and read "la fleur blanche." I repeated: "La fleur blanche! La fleur blanche! What a jolie fleur blanche you are . . ." I loved the French 'r,' which is pronounced like the Arabic letter ghayn. I tickled and caressed the letters in my mouth. Fleur! I felt I was diving deep and leaving my reality, inside the French ghayn. The things around me were no longer what they were. This isn't my room and my room is not in a basement, and the air conditioner doesn't drone, and the ceiling isn't filled with yellow blotches and the olive rug is a green meadow. I traveled. I traveled in language, without a passport and, more importantly, without a mahram—a male guardian.

Saqr sensed the wondrous chemistry that this language set off in me: the slowness in my mouth, the lightness of my steps, the shine in my eyes, my walk that was almost a dance. I was in love and everything I said and did betrayed me.

Every time he came down to the basement and found me stretched out on my back, French book in hand, courageously practicing the pronunciation of each word until it was just right, he would start complaining.

"Do you spend all day in front of that book?"

"I have a test," I'd lie. I would ignore other subjects just to read a line in French. I was discovering my passion.

"If you'd studied science like you study French now, your grades wouldn't have been so poor, mazmoizelle."

"*Mademoiselle*," I corrected him.

But he liked the first one better. He liked it specifically because it annoyed me, and he started repeating "Mazmoizelle . . . mazmoizelle." Then just "mazmaz," and finally, shortening and playing with the pronunciation so that it was alternately "maz," sour, and "mazza," appetizer.

Many other words fell victim to his sabotage attempts. 'Bonjour' became 'bon-sure,' 'bon-cure'; 'bonsoir' became 'bon-saw,' 'bon-paw.' Once when we were getting into the car he asked me how to say 'car' in French. I told him: "Voiture," and he told me I looked like I was about to throw up. From then on he started calling the black Lancer 'Foitoot.'

Day after day, word after word, Saqr ruined the beauty of French, poisoned it, walked all over it, and left its letters broken and bleeding in my mouth. Whenever he asked me about a word and I answered him, he did what he could to make it into a joke. Everyone would laugh, and I had to pretend to laugh with them and pretend to accept it, as if it didn't hurt.

In this world it was no longer possible for someone to study a beautiful language that is like music, whose words flow like streams and cleanse the soul. That was a luxury I didn't deserve. I wondered: If it was possible to travel through language, the way I traveled to the cafés of Paris, to its streets, sidewalks, and dark alleys when I repeated "la fleur blanche," if it's possible for a person to travel in a foreign language, could I travel in my mother tongue?

My old language was sad by nature, polluted by others, splattered with their mud. It sank under the burden of words locked up out of reach and a monopoly on truth that killed their unique meanings—this language, my language, could I refine it, recreate it, and claim it for myself alone? Could it be something that resembles me and speaks with my voice?

On that day I was, if only in my thoughts, very much a poet.

A Poet in Secret

I LAID MY HEAD ON the pillow. My chest was pounding as if I'd run miles. I was breathless and my vision blurred. I was panting after an impossible journey, like someone returning from Miraj. Buraq has gone and left me alone. I saw what I saw and no one will believe me. I was in a state of exultation and fear. I started repeating in a triumphant whisper: I wrote a poem! I wrote a poem!

What was I going to do, now that I'd written a poem?

I have to protect this small creature, this delicate and fragile thing. I have to protect its life no matter the cost. If Saqr found out about it, if he found out about my new relationship with language, he would ruin it. He would strangle my poems and steal their birds, he would dirty them with his hands that smell of fish, its letters would die as soon as he set his watchdog eyes loose on them, searching—never, I won't allow it!—for witnesses to the crime.

Saqr doesn't have to know about it, I thought. I won't let him come to me with another fatwa prohibiting the writing of poetry or the reading of novels. I won't allow him to sit with his legs propped up, fatwa in hand that he printed off the internet for a small service charge, and read to me the millionth lecture: The blessed sharia states that all doors to the temptations that lead to evil shall be closed, and the temptation of women is one of the greatest temptations men face. Thus we find in the two great books of hadith that the Prophet, God bless him

73

and grant him salvation, said, "I have left behind me no trial more harmful to men than women." For that reason the sharia blocks all roads to this temptation. Women are forbidden from traveling without a mahram; they are forbidden from being alone with a strange man, from allowing their beauty to be seen by them and from speaking to them with a softness of speech, along with other doors to temptation that the sharia has closed. There is no doubt that reading stories and poems goes against the purpose of the sharia because of the evil acts that it brings about, such as arousing natural impulses, paving the way for base fantasies and thoughts, and devoting time to things that are of no benefit to one's religion or the world, and are in fact harmful.

I can't let that happen. For him to seize hold of the one thing I have left, the one thing that I can do. I won't give him the chance! Since that first poem I decided to keep it all a secret, to get very good at hiding my writing before he could ruin it, before he could find out about it and start squashing my creations under his shoes.

If it was just about him tearing things up it would have been much easier, but his hostility was more subtle than that. He was the type that would take the journal hidden under your pillow and read it to everyone in the house until they were curled up on the floor in laughter. I imagine Saqr reading something I wrote, something like "That night my soul went out." He would be lying on his back, munching on sunflower seeds and spitting the shells everywhere, and he would read with a booming voice that was more than the delicate words could bear. Then he would ask, pretending to be dumb: Oh, so your soul went out. Are you a light bulb? And everyone would laugh and I would go to pieces. Throughout the following weeks everyone would call me "light bulb," and I would stop writing forever. This exquisite pleasure, extraordinary, that I'd just experienced a few minutes ago, it would disappear from my life.

I wrote my first poem on the bottom of a box of tissues. A short and disjointed poem, trembling like a tear, and I was happy with it, that tear poem, as if I'd stumbled upon myself.

I am a poet in secret. I write the silence and melt inside it. The world has no room for my poems.

I'll Repent When the Time Is Right

THE DEATH OF MY PARENTS didn't make me an orphan. I became an orphan when I didn't die, and when Saqr didn't die either. He remained in the world to become my jailer, to search my bags on the pretext of looking for gum, to scroll through my phone claiming he wanted to know if I had the number for Hardees, and to review my browser history on the computer to make sure I was not deviating from the course of virtue or talking to men in cyberspace. He guarded my honor like a dog, although a dog would have been more likable.

I found myself running away and returning in failure, without anyone knowing about it. The number of my graves would have just increased by one.

I wasn't able to be, to just be. To walk on God's earth without feeling that the world was going to prey on me. That's why I was always two steps ahead of him, through my symbolic death and my symbolic burial, by standing symbolically at my graveside and symbolically paying my last respects with flowers.

The flower seller knows me. He wraps my daisies with obvious care, and smiles too. When he smiles I think that he is one of the "human wolves" that Saqr talks about, who prey on girls. I never smiled back at him. Thanks to my brother the world was suspect, Saqr having claimed all honor for himself.

I want to be somewhere where there is room for people to be themselves, where what is outside resembles what is inside, where the two are in harmony with their truth—to study French, to draw birds, to write a poem in the daylight, to sit alone, to run in an amusement park, to touch the sea with their feet, to walk to the grocery store alone, to sit with their friends in a café. My own space, a space that belongs only to me, that harms no one, I want all of it. Why did they steal it? Why does the world invade me so?

To live in a place that seizes hold of every last centimeter of you means that you become skilled in the arts of evasion. I had to play tricks. To deceive. To dance my dance in the dark. I had to hide the files on my computer and protect them with a password so the guardian would not breach the secrecy of my poems. I had to download pirated books, save them on a flash drive, and read them without the guardian discovering my offense of reading outside the ideological curriculum and list of permitted readings. I had to reach my hand into the internet and pluck the fruits of the world and touch its vast spaces. I had to write under an assumed name, to put on masks in order to be my truth, to delete the browser history from the computer and erase my tracks on poetry websites and writing forums. To set my imagination free in my mind. To sit on the windowsill pondering the dust and calling it mist, to travel without leaving my place. To write delicate poems with no meter or rhyme because this type alone resembles me. To break the law that confiscated my humanity and taste the world outside. I steal away at night and practice running away.

Most importantly, I had to learn how to research different and conflicting opinions of sharia scholars. I developed a passion for fatwas, searching for gaps, openings, and holes where I might find a way through to points of view that differed from those that prevailed. Every time he said to me such-and-such thing is forbidden, I'd tell him scholar so-and-so has a different point of view. For hours I'd debate with him, test his knowledge, and try to force him to acknowledge that different opinions exist. I failed.

I had to lie. To go to the library and tell him that I was at the university. I sat in that deserted place, hidden in the rows of books. I would read, guarded by the spirits of the poets and philosophers, making friends with the characters in novels and living other lives.

I spent my whole life feeling that by reading I was committing a sin, and I was certain that if I died I'd have to spend some time in hell, as punishment for my disobedience, my undeclared outings, and the things I read in secret. I was doing the forbidden and the thought of hell terrified me, but I always promised myself that I would repent when the time was right—five minutes before I died.

The Gentleman

In Thailand. In the hotel.

I am outside the tomb. The tomb is inside me.

The hotel looks like a magical castle in an old fairy tale, surrounded by beautiful greenery that creates an enchanting halo around it. The smell of the sea in the air, relaxed faces and lowered voices, and orchids in every possible corner. Does there exist on earth a place dripping with this frightening fecundity? I pulled my hand from his and walked through the hotel and its passageways. I wanted to pick everything up with my eyes and hide it inside me.

I had to hide this place and save it, to put it in the empty jam jars under my bed so I could keep it. I was afraid the beauty would seep away. I felt my eyes filling with tears.

"Do you like it?"

"Are you kidding?"

I think I smiled for the first time since we'd gotten married.

"Thailand always amazes you" read the slogan printed at the bottom of the paper napkin in my hand. I nodded in agreement and decided to keep it. I folded it several times and hid it in the zipper pocket inside my bag, thinking, I'll collect so many napkins, I'll put them in empty jam jars, I'll save everything!

I moved like a sleepwalker. The hotel employee opened the door of our room with a white magnetic card and we entered. Leather sofas made of cane, a low table in the center of the salon, a twenty-inch television. On the white bedsheets pulled taut over the sides of the mattress they had made a heart out of red rose petals. On the television screen glowed the words: "Welcome, Mr. and Mrs. al-Farid."

The hotel employee politely lowered his head and excused himself after telling us that the resort was giving us a free reflexology session. I waited impatiently for him to leave so I could spread out on the wide bed and rest my cheek on the soft sheets. I lay down on my stomach, inhaled the scent of lavender from the sheets, and noticed the piece of chocolate resting on the pillow. I put it under my tongue and hid the wrapper in my bag. For the first time in many years I wasn't forced to close my eyes in order to see beauty.

Faris hopped onto the bed and its legs rocked like a ship in a storm. He laughed. I laughed too. He spread out on his back next to me. I pulled in my arms and legs and sat up. I started to get up. Stay, Fatima, he said. I have to go to the bathroom. Stay a little while. He laced his fingers between mine. My mouth went dry, my heart pounded. I looked at the window: what if I jumped now and ran?

"How long are you going to be so skittish?"

"I . . ."

"It's been three days. Three days!"

I said nothing.

"I'm a real gentleman, don't you think?"

He smiled vaguely. My eyes blurred. My heart retreated. Everything disappeared. Faris is a gentleman, a real gentleman. He waited three days. He's a real gentleman!

He picked up some rose petals and pressed them into my palm, then squeezed my palm in his hand.

"I like you."

He brought my palm close to his cheek, brushed it against his face, his chin, his neck. He felt like velvet.

"I'm lucky."

Faris is lucky, the pumpkin is ripe, the melon turned out to be sweet, the seller didn't cheat. He won the lottery.

The Prophet Said

MY LITTLE DREAMS FELL TO pieces in Saqr's hands, under the pretense that they were little. In seven years, Saqr stripped me of every personal trait, until I was no longer mine, until I was no longer me. The qualities that made me who I was, that mapped out my features and made me differ—as I pleased—from others. All were stolen, confiscated, became his property—though he cared nothing for them.

I wanted to study at the College of Arts. That would have been possible if my parents hadn't died.

I spent months with insomnia, anxiety. I was searching for a way to convince him to agree. I cried during prayers; I vowed the vows. I said, O God, grant me this small thing, grant me a place at the College of Arts. I need one beautiful thing in my life, one thing that I want. O Giver of Life, give me life.

For weeks I looked for a way to bring it up with him. When should I talk to him? At the dinner table his mind would be on his stomach, but that didn't mean it would be easier to get him to agree. He would simply say, Now is not the time. Maybe after he comes back from the mosque on Friday? He was usually happy. But what if he came back fired up on his obsession to control and push me to hate anything with life in it? Let alone study literature, a rich subject full of life. Should I wait? What was I waiting for? For him to lie back and prop his legs up while munching on salted pistachios? How could I convince someone who is completely convinced that he's got the truth tucked into his back pocket? How can I get through to him and make him see things with my eyes, with my heart, with my wounds and tears?

I knew I would have to support my request with arguments based on the sharia, and I started to search for them. I made a long list of every Quranic verse and prophetic hadith I could find. I forgot that Saqr didn't care about those verses and hadiths, but about what he called "the great sheikhs and scholars." Literature is nonsense.

One evening while he was watching a tennis match, I brought the subject up. I said, "This is my last year of secondary school and I want to study something I like in college."

"And what do you like, Mazmoizelle Fatima?"

"I like poetry."

"God save me." He spit out a shred of miswak that had gotten stuck between his teeth.

My heart retreated, my eyes blurred. I sensed where this discussion, which had ended before it began, was going.

He added, "*And the Poets, It is those straying in Evil, who follow them.*"

"*Not all of them are alike,*" I replied, quoting the Quran back at him. I got out my weapons, prepared to fight one authority with another. I added, "The Prophet said, In some eloquence there is magic, and in some poetry there is wisdom."

"Our scholars classify that as a weak hadith, and do not accept its authenticity. Nice try."

"Even if that's the case, isn't there truth in its meaning?"

"What do you know about what is true and what isn't true?"

"I have a mind that thinks."

"If you had any brains at all you would have studied something useful," he said, and spit out the shreds of miswak he'd crushed between his teeth. He got ready to leave. I followed him, held onto the stair railing as he went up, shaking it between my hands with all my might. I waved the paper, the list of arguments, everything I could find to support my position. I held onto the bottom of his white pants, shouting, "Kaab bin Zuhayr! Umayya bin Abi al-Salt! Antar! Al-Khansa! Hassan ibn Thabit!"

"What's wrong with you?"

"Poets! They're all poets!"

"That's enough. Conversation over."

"The Prophet loves poetry and you don't?"

"We're done talking about it. There will be no College of Arts. Women in this family don't go to mixed colleges. You have two solutions: study at the Girls' College or the Sharia College. Or you can plant yourself at home and wait for the ape that agrees to take you."

My heart clouded over, as I sank under the weight of the oppressive finality in his voice. I'd forgotten about the 'mixed gender' issue. I'd almost defeated him; I'd almost won a battle in the eternal war between the halal and the haram. I had almost scored a victory for poetry, for the image of the beautiful God who loves beauty. Tears flowed from my eyes as I sobbed.

"But, Hayat . . . Hayat . . ."

"What about Hayat?"

"Hayat is going to the College of Arts!"

"I don't like you being friends with her anyway."

"Hayat has been my friend since primary school."

"We're done talking about it. Or there will be no university. If you knew what's good for you, you'd shut up."

"But . . ."

He took two steps up, then turned to me and ended this weak, meaningless conversation, saying, "By the way, girls in this house don't go to university without wearing an abaya. If that's okay with you, good; if not, you can sit at home. And you don't need the diploma. You're a girl—someone else will take care of you."

You Talk Funny

WE WERE LYING ON THE bed. He was half naked and looked satisfied, his fingers playing lazily with my hair. I was curled up in a ball next to him, the covers pulled up to my neck. The television was on and the window was close, the sea far. My clothes were lying scattered around the room. I was filled with a strange sensation, as if I'd understood. I'd entered the secret area, the red zone that, it sometimes seemed to me, everything in this world revolved around. This was it then, what everyone was so excited about, what the books of virtue were filled with, what made men wolves and girls sheep or, at best, well-guarded "pearls" kept hidden in boxes, in a box inside a box inside a box, all in a closet with many locks, the closet in the basement and the basement a tomb. This then was the secret that made them work so hard to expel me from my life? What a disappointment!

Faris leaned on his right side with his palm on his cheek. "So you studied at the Girls' College?" he asked.

In this world, men sleep with a woman then get to know her.

"For three years."

"You never got a diploma?"

"No. Saqr decided that wasn't necessary. He said I would eventually get married, so what did I need a diploma for?"

"He has a point," he said, stretching and yawning lazily.

My stomach lurched. "Do you agree with him?"

"Well, actually, when I decided to get married I was look-ing for a girl who wouldn't mind being a housewife. Girls these days—"

"They're ambitious?"

"They crowd the men."

"Because after all, this world is your world?"

"Everyone has their role."

Just like that, this man who had taken me into his bed had decided what kind of life I should have. I closed my eyes, ready to sleep.

"But why aren't I given a chance to choose my role, based on what is right for me and what I am capable of?" I asked.

"All women are capable of doing housework."

"Men are capable of doing it too."

"Oh! A little revolutionary!" He pinched my cheek, as if he liked what I said. "You ask a lot of questions, like a child."

Then he kissed my palm. My fingers curled up. He laced them between his, and asked, "What did you major in?"

"Something related to computers."

"Why computers?"

"Because they are a window onto the universe."

"Computers are 'a window onto the universe'? Does any-one in the world really talk like that?"

"What do you mean?"

He yawned for the fourth time and said, "You talk funny."

I felt like I had some kind of deformity inside me. "I don't know any other way to talk." After a short silence I added, "I wanted to go to the College of Arts."

He didn't answer. Didn't ask. He closed his eyes, and after a while he started snoring. He wasn't interested in hear-ing the story.

My Adoptive Mother

AFTER WRITING MORE AND MORE, after many notebooks of thoughts and journals and poems that I didn't know at the time were poems, I understood that this spring that flowed from inside me would always be with me.

With writing, I was less an orphan. My mother had died, but language is a mother too. Language gave me many births, with every letter I wrote, and opened up horizons for me so that I might drink from her source, embrace her 'p's, and curl up inside her 'u's.

I'd take a word and peel off its skin, remove it from its context, ignore its history and where it came from. I'd make it clear and naked and an orphan, like me. Then I'd build from it a world. Language was my bread and water, the touch of my mother's palm and my father's broad chest. Language was everything, and I wrote it—everything.

I wrote and hid my writing in a box. The box was in a locked closet. To get a key you needed a blacksmith, to get a blacksmith you needed money, to get money you had to go to the bride . . . and the bride wanted a divorce.

The story was over before it began.

The Sea Is Not for Me

I AM NOT GOING WITH you. I said it just like that, planted on the couch in front of the television. I held my breath, ready for what came next. How would he behave when angry, this man who was now my husband? I'm not going with you. I'm not leaving this room. You can go alone if you want. I've had enough of going out. I want to stay here, in this lovely room. I want to collect all the papers and scraps and bits of fabric and hide them in jam jars.

"You go."

"What do you mean?"

"I'm not leaving here."

"You can't be serious."

"But I am."

"Don't you like the sea?"

"The sea is not for me."

Yesterday you said, You'll love the sea. Why wouldn't I love it? The sea deserves to be loved, and I would have loved it more, if it had been about more than me sitting on a beach chair for hours, drinking piña coladas and watching you swim—on your belly, on your back, on your side—before everyone: freestyle, the butterfly, the frog. The frog? Are you sure you didn't make these names up? Soaking wet, showing off in black swim trunks. You put the towel on your head and exclaimed, The water's amazing! Amazing! You quickly took a sip from your glass then went back, jogging. You went back in and I waited and watched. You waved to me, so I waved to you. It took tremendous effort to smile. Smiling exhausts me. I don't want to smile. I don't want to wave. This is a stupid game! You dove then your head came up and you shouted in disbelief, A sea turtle! A giant sea turtle!

"Well, I'm sure it's very exciting for you, the sea and the turtles and the sea urchins. . . . I'm sure you'll enjoy yourself a lot. But I . . ."

The long hours of sitting, gazing at your sheer delight, while starving inside. I smiled and waved like an idiot. I acted as if I were there, in the sea, with you. Me swimming and playing? You had said to me, It wouldn't be proper for you to go swimming. Your clothes would cling to your body. I'm a jealous husband. You said it like you were boasting.

A few years back, Saqr reprimanded me because I wanted to touch the sea with my foot. My bare foot. Today too I can't touch the sea or baptize myself in its waters, for the same reason, with the exception that you're not using the sacred as your crutch: you just decide and that's it. Nothing has changed. Only the beard is missing. I started looking at people and people looked at me, at my fully clothed body, at their fully naked bodies, the shiny, tanned, and oiled bodies, free as the sand and the wet sea air, the tropical palms, and the cocktail glasses. Even then I was still okay with things. If only, if only you hadn't waved your hand and pointed out, time after time after time—you in your swimming suit, with your firm torso and naked stomach—if you hadn't pointed at a lock of hair that had crept out of my hijab: Careful! Your hair is showing!

Faced with all your nakedness, faced with the irrationality of it all, I was furious and could no longer smile.

"You go. Have a nice time. I'll stay here. I'll watch a film."

Night Vigil

I COULDN'T SLEEP. I WASN'T despondent enough. Half despondent means half hopeful. It means that you think about the possibilities you missed out on in life. How you could have been different, and in a different place. What if things weren't the way they were? That "what if" opens the devil's door. "What if" is ruthless.

I wandered through the rooms. Opened the fridge three times. Emptied a carton of chocolate milk into my belly. I stood in front of the window for a long time, looking at the cats getting ready to pounce on each other, at the streetlights, the sidewalks, and the few cars passing by. There is always life somewhere.

I remembered when I used to knock on the door of my parents' room. Mama, I had a nightmare. Most likely I was lying. No nightmare, nothing of the kind. I wanted to sleep in the big bed. My mom was cheerful, as if she'd been waiting for me. She'd make a little space for me between her and my father. I'd stretch out between them, my mom holding my right hand and my father holding my left. Both of them slept on the side that was most comfortable for me, the side facing me. I'd grow sleepy in that little space of warmth. I'd rub my foot against my mom's. I'd wrap my father's arm around my stomach, my back to him. Slowly I'd fall asleep, ridiculously at peace, as if they would never leave. Things turned out a bit differently, I said to the reflection of my face in the window, a wry smile on my face. Who's the most miserable one of all?

Maybe I should read until I get sleepy. Invent a substitute for that nighttime embrace, an antidote to the insomnia and nightmares. The nightmare was my reality and it was impossible to sleep. As if sleeping were waking, and waking the punishment. I was getting ready to go back down when I heard a laugh. Who was laughing now? Who could laugh at two in the morning, while everyone was asleep?

Wadha? Was Wadha laughing, having convinced everyone she had been in bed since nine? I went upstairs, on tiptoe, to her room. The door was half open. Why had she left it like that? Was it an oversight, overconfidence, or extreme caution? I pressed my back to the wall next to the door and listened. She was laughing! She was laughing on the phone, a laugh impossible to misinterpret, whose coyness had but one meaning. There was a scandalous femininity and overt desire in her hesitations. She whispered, implored, Come on now! Knock it off, or I swear I won't indulge you again!

I was in my basement in a minute, shaking as if it were all my fault. This then was the nocturnal world of the perfect daughter? Everything else she did, her death-defying courage in pleasing and impressing Saqr, was to give herself—when everyone was asleep—suitable cover to laugh her sinful laugh in the late-night hours?

In the morning her mother asked her about the traces of fatigue on her face. Didn't you get enough sleep? You were in bed at nine! Wadha touched her forehead wearily, lowered her eyes in great modesty, and like a devout worshipper who fears appearing to be seeking praise replied, "I was up last night praying."

Wine

THAT DAY IT WAS BECAUSE he found the word 'wine' in a book I was reading. Saqr lost it. In his eyes, that was enough to earn me forty lashes.

He snatched the book from me and tore it up, then threw it at my feet. I watched as the characters of the novel raced around, clear as day, terrified by the sudden attack. I saw the carnage, the arms and the legs and the heads severed from their bodies, the orphaned shoes flying in the air. Everyone was wiped out. I started gathering up the papers, apologizing. I buried them together in an empty flowerpot in the courtyard of the house, making them a mass grave.

Another day Saqr happened to come by my room on one of his patrols while I was reading Charles Baudelaire's *Le Spleen de Paris*. I was feeling out the magical form of the prose poem, born without head or tail. Saqr took the book.

"What's this?"

He held the book by its cover as if he were holding a bird by its wings.

"Poetry."

"So this is the latest thing now?" He spoke with great disdain. I didn't want to say a word in front of him. My focus was on how to avoid a confrontation and get rid of him as quickly as possible.

"God, people have nothing better to do."

"Well, I finished my homework, so I don't really have anything better to do."

"Go read a few verses from the Quran. That would be better for you and serve you better in the afterlife."

He won't let me love anything in this world, I thought sadly.

"Reading isn't haram. The Quran tells us to read."

"We read the Quran, not the heretical ramblings of Baudelaire and Voltaire and junk like that."

"The Prophet said, 'A believer is always seeking wisdom, wherever it is found.'"

"We Muslims don't need any more wisdom."

"If that's true, then why are we a backward ummah?"

"Because we chase breathlessly after the heretical ramblings of unbelievers."

Heretical ramblings of unbelievers. He said it with so much loathing. It seemed the words had worked their effect on him, because in no time he grew enraged and started ripping the book up before my eyes, as if he were tearing the feathers from the wings of a bird, the bird trembling in fear. Then he threw it on the ground, declaring, "You'll thank me one day, even if that isn't until Judgment Day."

After that, I started downloading pirated books from the internet and having them printed and bound at the student services center with clear plastic covers and titles like *Negotiation Skills 221* by Dr. Ounsi al-Hajj, *Introduction to Political Science 101* by Dr. Mahmoud Darwish, *Computer Systems Management* by Dr. Amin Salih.

It cost me around nine dirhams to have a book made, including paper, ink, and binding. It was so easy it was funny, and it made me feel superior. I'd fooled my big brother! My impossible brother, as huge as the wall and the closets and the rain boots. I beat him.

Titanic

You'll like it. It was a huge success in America. He put a bag of M&Ms in my hand when he said it. You ready? Let's go. He had been excited since he found out I hadn't gone to a movie in seven years. For some reason I wasn't excited. I was nervous, afraid I'd do something wrong. What could a person do wrong at the movies? I hung onto his arm as we walked. I went up the steps in the dark, my heart pounding in my ears. I really am here, Saqr can't touch me. I was thinking about Saqr, not the film, and that was unfortunate. I remembered Hayat, remembered that night.

We'd been on the phone for three hours, awake after everyone had gone to bed, so she could tell me about the movie that was taking the world by storm, winning eleven Oscars—*Titanic*. The sea and love and death and drowning. I listened for three hours while Hayat told the story. She described the burgundy dress covered in black lace and crystal beads, the scene where they stood on the edge of the ship, Jack the gambler and Rose suffocating under the pressure of a life forced upon her and controlled by someone else. She described the moment when Rose stood on her tiptoes and was raised off the ground as if she were flying. "She really was flying, Fatima!" Hayat swore to me. "Do you think it was a special effect?"

"I don't know, Hayat."

"Maybe they raised her up on a string."

"Did you see a string?"

"Even if there was a string, you think the director would let it show?"

"I don't know."

"They aren't careless about stuff like that."

"Who?"

"The Americans. They take movies very seriously."

"How would I know that?"

"Well, you know now, I'm telling you."

After three hours of hearing the story told down to the very last detail I found myself crying.

"Fatima, what's wrong?"

"Nothing."

"Why are you crying? Are you sad Jack drowned?"

"No."

"Then why are you crying?"

"I miss my mom."

I was an orphan. It was so obvious—it was phosphorescent—and glaring me in the face.

After that Hayat didn't tell me about the films she saw, and if I asked her she'd wave with great indifference and say, Oh . . . it was boring, you're lucky you didn't waste your time on it. That's how Hayat fought my orphanhood.

The movie started. Faris wrapped his arm around the back of my seat. Slowly he got closer and closer. He wanted to sit comfortably with his arm around my shoulders. That is, for me to feel comfortable with his arm around my shoulders, for us to get comfortable with each other. My body stiffened. I pretended to be a piece of wood, a piece of wood watching a movie, while his hand started searching for my fingers, squeezing them together, touching my skin gently, filling me with questions: why can't I accept this man's love?

A Bad Apple

STANDING IN THE MIDDLE OF the hallway at the Girls' College in Adailiya, facing each other, Hayat and I are fighting. Our voices rise and our hands wave in the air. She says, "You're comfortable being a victim!"

"How could you say such a thing?"

"I have to be honest with you."

"To be honest with me?"

"Yes."

"You, in your perfect world, without any problems?"

"I say what I see!"

"Who are you to judge?"

"I'm the only person in the world who has the right to tell you something like this."

I sighed. Tears escaped from my eyes. I wiped at them with the sleeve of my abaya while gazing enviously at her light-blue shirt. I love your shirt and I hate my abaya.

"I know how hard life at your brother's house is," Hayat says, "but I also know that you can fight, and you don't."

When Hayat speaks you feel the world is speaking through her.

"I'm still . . ."

"It's not enough! We always meet at your school. I always come to you. You're too much of a coward to disobey him."

She can see the life in me drying up and slipping away, and she demands more from me. Saqr, who always senses her insistent voice when it erupts from within me, has repeated to me many times that she's "a bad influence," without sufficient facts or evidence or proof. Looking at my face was enough to establish suspicion. Hayat supplies me with will. One follows their friend's religion, as the hadith says, and Hayat was a bad apple. Bad apples make all the apples rotten.

"You don't come over to my house anymore. Is being with me somehow disgraceful? Have you become like them?"

Whenever Hayat asked me to come over to her house I made excuses, because Saqr didn't approve. He'd say, I'm not comfortable with Hayat or how she's been raised. She'd say to me, I'll come over to your house. So I'd say, Saqr won't allow it. It was a lie; I didn't want her to see the basement and lose what dignity I had left.

"If you can sneak out at night to bury flowers, why don't you use that time to sit with me in a café? What's stopping you?"

Ever since he found out that she studies "foreigner" literature, as he called it, Saqr won't allow me to go shopping with Hayat or go to a café with her, even if her family is there. He kept saying that she will ruin my morals. Hayat was a bad apple.

"I'm holding on to our friendship with all my strength, but you don't make it easy."

Hayat was the struggle and the hand that always reached out with a flower or song. She was constantly besieging me with questions: Who would know if you went to a morning poetry reading? A photography exhibition? If we went shopping together? How would he find out? If he found out what could he do? He can't turn back time and take away your fun.

"Your chains aren't that tight, you can slip out of them sometimes. If you can get an extra inch, then do it. And if you don't, shame on you."

She always said that I overestimated his power. That's easy for you to say, I would answer defensively.

Hayat studies English literature without anyone accusing her of trying to be a Westerner or of being bewitched by the unbelievers. She reads Shakespeare and Virginia Woolf and Charles Dickens without being forced to tear off the book covers and hide the pages under the pillows. At Hayat's house, a person can love life without being accused of having been taken in by a world that is not worth the wing on a gnat before God. At Hayat's house, the world is sweet and fresh.

"I didn't create this vast distance between us."

"Neither did I."

Before my parents died, I could barely make out the differences between her life and mine. We bought the same things, from the same stores. We loved the same things, the same colors. We tried to eliminate as many differences as possible in the hope that we would become one. The strict rules we invented to protect this friendship required, for example, that we come to school with a ponytail on Saturday, a French braid on Sunday. That our favorite color was pink. That we buy the same schoolbag for the semester, along with other things to make us more alike. That was well before my parents died. The difference—after all that—hurt.

"You like your new friends more than me. They don't have older brothers like Saqr."

After we started college Hayat made other friends. Who could blame her? Did I dare? I was a friend from a faraway college and harsh disappointments. I was a real burden. And as for her, she had Shaymaa and Rawiya and Zaynab, friends who could go to the movies with her, go over to her house. They could go shopping with her and sit in cafés with her and go to all kinds of social events—parties, weddings, birthdays . . . All the fruits forbidden to me in the name of keeping me in that hell he called my paradise.

"That's not true."

"Yes it is."

"Lately all I see is me running after you. Do something for me."

"What do you want me to do?"

"Come with me tomorrow."

I sniffed, wiping my tears with the edge of my abaya. "Where?"

"To a poetry reading. In Kaifan. 12:30 p.m. I'll come pick you up."

Hayat's a bad apple? Maybe I should be a bad apple, so I don't get eaten up.

Your Poet

IT WAS A SMALL AUDITORIUM, because poetry isn't a hot commodity, because poetry isn't a commodity. We sat in the first row. For the first time in my life I was going to listen to poetry read in someone else's voice, while I melted into the language. There were three men and one woman, all students, who'd come from different colleges carrying their notebooks and white papers, to read their poetry to us. They all looked similar, except for one. Only one set his fragility on the table, proclaiming his human weakness, said, I'm afraid, I'm nervous, I'm wounded. I can't hold it together, the music in my poetry is heard by the soul and not the ear. They came armed with the violins of language and its lofty strings, and he had the throat of a bird; he read as if his mouth frightened him. He was skinny, balding, and had shaved off the rest of his hair. He had a wide forehead, two pairs of glasses with black frames, golden skin, deep-set eyes, and thick eyebrows that arched beautifully as if they carried the weight of the world. His lips were thin and his mouth dry. He wore an olive shirt that was the color of the carpet in my room, and on his right eyebrow was a cut that looked like the crack in my wall. He looked like my life and my life looked like him; his poetry overflowed with orphanhood and exile, although he wasn't really an orphan, nor completely exiled. When he read his poetry, I felt that he made the disaster concealed inside me speak. The unsettling electricity between us was something supernatural and extraordinary. I think I was the only one who listened to him that morning. He spoke to me as if he were my mouth.

Everyone had finished—he had been the last. The sparse audience clapped and everyone started gathering their things and getting ready to leave.

"Was it worth coming?" Hayat asked me.

"Definitely!"

She nudged my arm, feeling victorious.

"You should always do as I say."

"It seems I will."

"What did you think?"

"About what?"

"Everything."

"The last one was the best."

"You mean Isam?"

"I think that's his name."

"He's mysterious. I didn't understand his stuff."

I smiled, as if happy to possess exclusive understanding of him.

I started to feel anxious. "Let's go, before the driver arrives. If I'm late it'll be the end of the world."

"Don't worry. . . . We'll go back soon."

We had started to leave when she commented, "Look at your poet. Poor guy, no one is talking to him!"

Each of the participants had a group hovering around them asking questions and congratulating them. Except him.

Hayat pulled my hand and said, "Come, let's say hi." Crazy Hayat, she does things like that with the naturalness of a mother who doesn't want to discourage the poet whose "stuff" she "didn't understand" and he. . . . Was he looking at me? I stood silent as a wall next to Hayat, who started to praise him at length and told him that she wished to read more of his work, lots of other things, lovely and untrue and fueled by good intentions. She ended by telling him simply, "My friend is a poet too!" He raised his eyebrows, and my heart skipped a beat. This time he looked right at me, right at my heart, which had been taken by surprise. I felt exposed and my heart pounded. "I—I'm not a poet," I stammered. "I scribble."

"I love scribbles."

He said it and smiled. Then he wrote his email on the back of his poem, pressed the paper into my hand, and left. My body started to shake. "What's wrong with you?" Hayat asked. I didn't know how to respond. I was shaking like I had a fever.

"It's cold."

Hours later I was crouched in the depths of the basement, in the deepest pit of my soul. I inhaled the traces of the sweet perfume that had penetrated my life that afternoon. Happiness spread inside me. I said to myself, I want to draw out the experience, I want the poem to continue forever, stretching out between two mythological banks, like a rainbow. I will send him a message now, I will fight for myself and send him a message I'd written on a scrap of paper, folded and folded, then hid in a honey jar, hiding the jar under my bed. Poetry is a box inside a box, I pry open its secrecy and pull it gently from the hidden pouch, from inside the belly of a whale, from the heart of certainty. I turned the computer on, entered his email address, and in the great white space my fingers raced to type my four brief lines:

My heart is a black hole
Sucking everything in
I am the crushing mouth of nonexistence
I am the end of the world.

The Slap of Dreams

I USED TO WISH HE'D slap me and that would be it.

I prayed hard for that slap.

I called it the slap of my dreams.

If he'd gone so far as to slap me, I would have been able to point my finger at him and say he's cruel. If his animosity toward me had been overt, I would have been able to hate him without hesitation, without feeling I was rotten inside, full of ungratefulness and overflowing with lies. If he'd raised his hand and slapped me I would have given up, perhaps, on trying to fit into a world of such illusion and barrenness, and on calling those attempts getting closer to God. I would have felt less guilt. I would have liked myself more.

But he didn't. And I—I avoided him for seven years. I snuck out of the house and returned, the way a bird with clipped wings goes back to its cage, because the sky is so much bigger than it.

I needed that slap to believe I was his victim. I thirsted for it and prayed to God for it, the slap of my dreams, the slap that would be the end. When would it come? And why wasn't he more transparent, more manly, in his hostility toward me? Rather than repeating that my voice was "out of tune" every time I hummed a little. Rather than telling me my face was funny looking, and that when I smiled I looked like a schizophrenic. Or constantly saying that I was a ripe banana no one wanted, that I wasn't smart, wasn't competent to read or think. That I was much less than I would need to be in order to earn his approval in anything. If I wasn't capable of pleasing him, he who was just an older brother, how would I please God in His heavens?

I took his words as divine revelation, given his beard and the miswak in his mouth. In my mind, Saqr spoke the truth, a truth that filled me with pain and sapped my strength. He was like rust upon my heart, and I could no longer make out the right path. I was lost.

O Lord, bring him to slap me, a strong and resounding slap on my right cheek. Dispel the nightmare, and throw me into the living hell. I prayed again and again. For years I prayed to God to make his hand rise and slap me, so I could be freed.

I never imagined that this would really happen, and that it would happen in front of an audience of professors and friends, at my first poetry reading.

Inbox

Isam:

I think you feed straight from the wound.

Why don't you send me more poetry?

Don't worry, I'm a good swimmer.

And . . . what's your name?

You have to tell me. Otherwise I'll call you The End of the World, The Crushing Force of Nonexistence, other nice names like that. Arthur Rimbaud called his mother the "Mouth of Darkness." Do you know your poem is like that same mouth? The Mouth of Darkness?

I'm not afraid of the dark.

So. What's your name?

Isam:

Why don't you write back?

Are you mad?

How do you look when you're mad? Do your ears get red?

Do you break dishes, or wash them?

Tell me.

Fatima:

I live inside the poem. From here the world seems an illusion.

You're part of this illusion, and illusions frighten
me more than facts.

I live cut off from everything, in a mythical underground tomb.

I've weaned the child inside me.

That is my name.

Isam:

Gently now, Fatima.

Before you leave . . .

Give me another poem.

Isam:

I've been waiting for you here for two hours. This is
a farce.

It's clear you play the silence well.

How many hours do you practice a day?

Tell me something I don't like so I can forget all this.

I want to turn off this damn computer, it's hot and
irritated with me.

And you.

Fatima:

What do you want?

Isam:

I want what a poet wants from a poem. I want to love
poetry through you.

I want to throw you, write you, cry you, tear you
up, fathom you, travel in your blood.

I want to inhabit you.

Sometimes I kiss my poems.

Sometimes I burn them.

It depends on how beautiful they are.

What I want from you is everything.

Fatima:
> Very moving.
>> I almost believed you.

That was the last message.

A Clarification

I WAS SPLIT IN TWO, a question planted at my waist. I spent six months feeling torn.

My mind was assuring me that I'd just escaped. My heart was saying, No, you perished.

During those months I grew less rigid. My heart started to reject my excuses, one after the other. If he was a bad guy, if he was a 'wolf,' the insult wouldn't have hurt him. I'd blocked him with the point of my pen, with a precise hit right where it would hurt the most: his poem.

My caution had won out, even though inside I was starved for his words. All men were suspect, that's what Saqr said. Every man was a 'wolf' and every girl a 'sheep.' Caution was necessary. In the end, my older brother might be right.

In those dark, solitary nights, I started gazing into the gloom around me and reviving the memory, setting aside some tenderness as provisions for the future. I wondered if he was thinking about me too, if he still remembered me, if, despite my presumptuousness and my silence, I meant to him what he meant to me.

It was all the beauty and tenderness I could have hoped for in this barren life. Despite my obstinacy, my refusal, and my stubbornness, I didn't doubt that for a moment. I found myself hugging my pillow tightly while reliving the day I met him, the day he read his poem and his eyes looked into the depths of my soul, those frighteningly deep eyes. A night of music and secrets, emptied into my soul.

I thought about him every day for six months, until I felt that I knew him. I read his letters over and over and felt so happy. I relaxed. The thick skin that protected me from the world fell away. It's okay if you let your guard down just a bit, I told myself. If I took a risk and exposed myself to another blow, what did I have to lose?

Every time I read his odd question about the color of my ears when I get mad I felt like the luckiest girl. For years I'd lived in this house without anyone caring what I felt, what I needed, if I had dinner before I went to bed or not. Now this strange man came and asked me about something I didn't know myself. Do my ears get red when I'm mad?

The man was so interested in me that he'd studied me, dissected me inside and out, something that exceeded my wildest fantasies. I closed my eyes and imagined him over and over, little pieces torn from a picture: his hand holding the doorknob, the sweat on his brow, an eyelash on a cheek, a scar on the eyebrow and a scab on the right knee, a slight limp, black coffee. Many things—I wasn't sure if I'd made them up or seen them with my own eyes.

Six months went by with me holding on to him inside me, like a secret, like a sin, like a poem, like the one thing that made life possible. I hid him in my eyelids, provisions for my soul, and whenever the world got too nasty, I'd take him out of the pocket of my heart, like a talisman.

I could have been satisfied with what I'd had, a quick succession of letters, a relationship that ended before it began, with the electricity in my body, the narcotic buzz at the edge of poetry. I could have been satisfied, I could have thanked God for giving me five messages that made me believe life could be different.

Six months went by.

Isam:

Listen to this story.

This is the story of a poet who decided to write a story. Because he doesn't know how to write stories, he's going to say to you what his grandmother said to him: once upon a time.

Once upon a time there was a poet who decided to write a story.

He's writing it now.

Once there was a poet no one read, a poet no one saw. He decided to participate in a silly event and sit on a silly stage. That day, poetry got confused with pottery. The poet was unseen and paying the price of his idiotic decisions in a seven-meter-square seminar room at a university. There were eleven people, ten of whom the poet didn't see. He just saw one, only one, the one who saw him, the one who made him seen.

From that moment, the story has had another character.

Now we have the poet and the one.

The poet read his poem, and he felt something that hadn't happened before—that the words were coming out of his mouth and taking form in the space around him. They had height and width and length, scent and meaning and music. He saw, to his great wonder, the words of his story flowing down the cheek of the one and settling in the pores of her skin. He saw that his words were more comfortable with her than they were with him, she loved them more than he, they flew to her, they sat on her fingertips, nestled in her eyelashes, refusing to leave. For the first time, the poet saw that the words that left him didn't die, but were reborn. He was finally convinced that he was who he thought he was, and for the first time in his life he believed the voice inside him that told him he was a poet.

The one approached the poet after the people had left, and even though she didn't say anything special, he felt the whole universe was on his side. It was giving him the one who made him seen and a poet at once. He was sure of himself, very sure, because he saw it as a sign that the world was on his side for the first time and was giving him something he wanted, giving him the one. When he found out that the one was a poet, he thought it was too good to be true, and said he had to see it with his own eyes. When she sent him a poem she'd written, just four lines long, he could sense deep caves within her, tugging at his ears to enter, and said to himself, She's not just pretty, she writes poetry that is like a knife.

It's true, the poet thinks the one is pretty. Now, after this silly clarification, let's finish the story.

The one didn't expect the poet to make such silly, clownish leaps, to write to her as if he's known her for years, longed to know her for years. She's right, it's not logical. She thought that the poet was exaggerating and lying. When did you suffer so? she asked. When?

It seems she didn't pay close enough attention to him. He's a poet and doesn't need a long time to understand the things he's drawn to. But he sent her silly stuff, thinking he was being funny. He did things wrong, even though his intentions were very good, and today he's writing this story, his story, after six months of obstinacy and stubbornness, to say one thing: I'm sorry, Fatima.

Isam

Fatima:

Dear Isam,

I don't know if anger makes my ears turn red.
I'd nearly forgotten I have ears.

I don't break dishes,
Or wash them.
When my face breaks in the mirror,
I feel my insides are out.

The glass vessel of my spirit is cracked.
Writing is a glue:
It pulls me together,
Saves me just in time,
And leaves me to perish.

I just write.
I write my slight poems on the bottom of a box of tissues,
A precautionary measure against any attack on my notebook.
The things I write are like me,
I am out of tune.

Isam:
Dear Fatima,
A small vein on my thumb swelled from writing so much. Then it divided in two and became something resembling the place where the Tigris and Euphrates meet. Since that day I've been happy with the Iraqi river on my finger. I raise it to the world and call out to the gulf: "O Gulf! O giver of shells and death." Al-Sayyab swells in my blood.
When I do that, my mother laughs. My father says, The boy's gone mad.
I say to him, "And if the boy were a stone?"

I write on unlined paper,
I shake the rhymes loose,

I step on the meter of poetry and celebrate its
pure glow.

My question for you today is:
Have you always written your poetry like this,
flowing and loose?

Good morning, Fatima.

Fatima:
Good morning, Isam.
On the table where I sit now there's a computer
screen, a ripe banana, books with their covers torn
off, antibacterial wipes, cracker crumbs, and a dead
ant. If things can be like this, comfortable with their
strangeness, having no problem being next to each
other despite all their differences, then I want my
writing to be like this table. The world deconstructed
and confused.

Rhyme and meter are not because of my confu-
sion or fragility.
I break into pieces along the lines, trembling as
I walk.
The poetry I know does not resemble poetry as
generally recognized;
It's more ambiguous.

Once when my brother read a line of Baudelaire
He laughed out loud and asked, So this is the
latest thing now?

He's right.
I belong to the last latest thing.
The thing five minutes before the world ends.

The poetry I write is like the seedling you plant before the final hour.

My brother still curses cars and praises the camel. I don't know which of us is right.

Yes, I've always written like this.

Whenever the cell closes in, the poem expands.

Isam:

Good evening, Fatima.

I know a poet who wrote his memoirs in prison and smuggled them out in his underwear. Later he discovered that what he'd written was poetry. I don't know him, as in *know* him, I've just read everything he wrote, this poet who discovered poetry like Newton discovered the laws of gravity. Have you heard of him? Muhammad al-Maghout, his fear and his poetry? You seem to be like him, Fatima.

It frightens me that you're so real that you find inside yourself poems in their most primal form. You write as though extending your hand to the forbidden tree, evoking the tragedy of the first man, his fall and fright.

As for me, I've always had to repeat the words of Suzanne Bernard and Baudelaire, to memorize Rimbaud's "Letters of the Seer," to cite Ounsi al-Hajj and Qasim Haddad. I've always had to justify the chaotic form of my poems, for there are, it seems, rights to everything, even poetry.

I searched for my supposed 'legitimacy' in the wrong world, trying to convince people who don't read that poetry can exist anywhere, even in prose.

You, Fatima, didn't have to do any of that, you write your essence, you discovered for yourself, from your cell, that your heart is the philosopher's stone.

By the way . . . when you say 'cell,' do you mean
a *cell*? A *prison* cell?

Fatima:

Cell Block No. 13

Between Zayd's cell and Amr's cell.
Because those characters from our grammar books
are still hitting each other. . . .

There's a fan hanging from the ceiling
by a noose.
No one thought of giving it
a proper funeral.
We also have
a Mitsubishi air conditioner
drooling on the wall.
The wall doesn't mind;
it's just getting full of cracks.

My books are naked.
I ripped off their skin,
promising to cover them with floral wrapping paper,
which I never did.

Mahmoud Darwish's *Mural*
has been covered with white printer paper.
On the sticker I wrote:
"Introduction to Automated Systems 101."

At 9 p.m.
I have to turn off the computer
until the sun rises.
My brother says
that's when the devils come
to computers with the lights on.

Because cyberspace
turns into a bar.
I say to myself:
If I were Cinderella
I would have three more hours
until the spell is broken
and the ball ends.

I am not Cinderella.

When I say 'cell,'
this is exactly what I mean:
a prison cell . . .
"Big Brother is watching you."

Isam:
It's one in the morning.
Fatima, where are you?
I'm weak, wasted, the cold is killing me.
Where did you go? Are you asleep? How can you
sleep like this?
Are you dreaming? Of whom? What about me,
traitor?

How do you look when you're sleeping? Do you
rest your forearm over your eyes? Do you leave your
mouth half open? Do your eyelids flutter? Do you
leave your top button open? Do you sleep on your
right side or your left, or on your stomach? How do
you look right now? Tell me!
I want to be more than I am. I need to sneak
in through the air-conditioning vents, dig a trench
with a spoon, a trench so I can reach you, sit on the
side of your bed and look at you, at your fluttering

eyelids, I really must see how your eyelids flutter. I want to take you all in, Fatima.

I'm thinking about you and you're asleep, the acids burning my stomach.

The world is unjust. I'm thirsty and hungry and can't sleep, Fatima, and you're asleep.

It's not fair for me to be here and you there.

Damn you.

Isam:

It's four in the morning.

I wanted to tell you I still haven't slept.

Isam:

Six in the morning.

I read our twenty messages over and over.

Am I Don Quixote?

Fatima:

It's 7 a.m., I don't have much time.

My first class begins at eight and I have to hurry.

I just wanted to tell you that, like you, I didn't sleep,

But I'm not complaining or cursing.

I'm grateful for my insomnia.

Good morning, Poet.

Isam:

I don't know what has come over me.

I have some kind of disorder.

I'm no longer satisfied with a message. I wait for you in front of this computer for hours, and hate that I'm waiting for you.

Tell me about your day, tell me about you.

There are a lot of details missing from the picture.

I need you to fill in the blanks, so I can understand what's going on inside me.

I need to know more than your name. What do you study? What's your favorite toothpaste? How do you feel about earthworms? What TV shows do you watch? Do you write on paper or type directly onto the computer?

Do you have a pair of orange pajamas? I've had this damn pair of orange pajamas stuck in my head since yesterday, where did they come from? Tell me.

Do your hands smell like mint? Cardamom? Oud? Musk? Bouillon? Anything. What's your favorite perfume, so I can buy it, so I can pour it on my pillow, so I can love whoever made it. So I can be jealous of him. Kill him.

There are so, so many blanks. Be nice and fill them in for me. Come on.

Fatima:

I'm less than you think.
    I am full of blanks, all across and down,
    A chessboard.

Every time you do something nice,
    The uglier the world seems.

I'm afraid to get used to you. Afraid I won't.

Isam:

I was watching a movie.
    The movie was about a sailor.
    The sailor took a map out of a drawer and put it on the table.
    The map folded back up into itself.

125

I've figured it out, Fatima.
You're a map.
Why do maps fold up into themselves?
That's what I'm going to find out.
I'm a sailor.

Isam:

"Fatima, O dust of the stars, you left me
Carousing with them all night—and, you, without
regret.

Let me drink from the milk of your mouth, lost,
This one whose heart circles the spring.

Were it not for the impossible, you'd not find me here,
Cut off, thirsting for you, the girl named Fatima."

Isam:

Fatima,
Just how much can a poet love you—
Say, "I love you"—
Without you curling up into yourself
Like this?

Fatima:

Just how much can a person stare into the abyss?

We shouldn't let love happen.
Love is a crime, and a punishment.
A punishment for what? For the crime of allowing
love to happen. How can a sin like this be allowed to
occur, to pollute the place, muddy its purity, and draw
it out of its compulsory monasticism and self-denial,
its unbearable emptiness?

Love is life's response to life. Life's response to the voice inside. Life's nature is to live.

How can love not be a crime when it is a response to a call? A rebellious revolt against nonexistence, a response to life's lowly flower despite its inevitable end and its pitiable shortness of years.

How could we allow it?

"Of Love—may God exalt you . . ."

Don't bother, Ibn Hazm. They don't read.

Isam:

Good evening, Lovely,

Today I got a call from the writers' group. They never stop sending invitations or holding readings or planning more and more poetry nights. We have dozens of writers' groups in Kuwait, and no readers. Depressed by your disconcerting reply, I told myself that I'd go to today's meeting. Maybe I'd remember what the world was like before you. Maybe I'd love you less.

Sitting there, mug in hand, my coffee black the way I like it, my whole body sunk deep into the leather couch at our usual café, The Coffee Bean. I listened, bored with that meaningless and unending discussion about the legitimacy and illegitimacy of the prose poem. Everyone was holding a book of poetry by Dorianne Laux in their hand, and Dorianne Laux was bored and sad like me.

I realized that I was no longer myself. This subject in particular, that I used to swim in with all my critical muscle and everything I've ever read, was no longer at all appealing. Poetry was real to me in a way it hadn't been before, and real things don't need official recognition from the relevant authorities.

If only Fatima were here, I thought, with me, in this chair next to me. If only she were sitting on my right, shy and withdrawn, working hard to hide the universe in her heart. What if you were next to me, Fatima? What if our knees touched accidentally—or perhaps intentionally? What if I could get through this fake icy shell in which you wrap your true presence? If only. If only.

My hand shook and my coffee flew in the air.

My shirt will testify to my guilt.

Fatima:

I have an hour before the internet is turned off.

This is the last thing I'll write to you today.

Here in cell block No. 13 the guards have started to notice something different about me, something I failed to attend to. Did I tell you about the guards before? About the poem patrol? About the campaign to send the poem to the gallows, about the regime's mercenaries?

I am hounded by questions. They swarm around me, float over my head like a turban of smoke. Where there is smoke there is fire, says the patrol, certain of the sin before it has been committed: what are you waiting for and why do your eyes shine like that? What is it about your walk that has changed? Why are you standing up so straight, why are you flushed?

Happiness is suspect.

I was dying of jealousy when I read your letter—a café, poetry, Dorianne Laux? I almost envy you.

Be grateful for the coffee and friendship and the group and Dorianne Laux. Reading the most basic things in your letter—your ability to go out, to feel bored, to join a discussion about poetry, to let your body sink into a giant couch—all of this, these beautiful things, make me feel that I am dead.

My sadness is as long
As the night that sobs in my chest.
I wish you hadn't written to me.
I wish I hadn't been born.

Isam:

I'm going to get mad at you, Fatima. I'll get mad even
if you retreat, turn, and fold up into yourself like a
map, like an earthworm, like a damn hedgehog. I'll
get mad at you and for you and with you! I'll be hard
on you, out of love for you, Fatima.

Your message makes me feel I don't know you
and this makes me mad. I know we've only been writing to each other for a few days, but I have a right to
be angry at you. I want to know all of you.

I know that I know your inner truth, your profound
truth. I know your essence, and I close my eyes and
imagine that I've worked my way into your pores, that
I slip through your veins. I sit comfortably in the right
pocket of your heart and feel there is nothing I don't
know about you. At the same time I know nothing about
your situation, and you write to me about a "mythical
tomb" and about "cell block No. 13" and about the
Mitsubishi air conditioner and . . . for a moment I imagine—forgive me—that you're speaking metaphorically.
Then. Then I read you like this, so unexpectedly, in a
different way. Suddenly I see another truth. I see—I see
your pain, Fatima, I feel it, I hold it in my hand and feel
it, hot, burning my fingers. I feel that you are in pain and
still you don't find it in you to write to me, to vent, to rest
your head on my shoulder, on the shoulder of my poem.

I love you, Fatima, my miserable Fatima.
Further than you can go in a poem.
I'm mad.

Fatima:

Good morning, O poet,
>O gulf,
>O river,
>Splendid giver of shells and poetry.

I have a class in an hour and a half.
I am a student at the Girls' College, which is not what I wanted.

I will learn with you, from you, how to vent . . .
I will vent, open up, speak, disclose, complain, open my mouth.
I started today:
I'm a student at the Girls' College and that wasn't what I wanted.
The end.

Isam:

A student at the Girls' College? Eight lines to tell me you study at the Girls' College?
At this rate it's going to take me three or four years to learn everything I want to know about you.
Speaking of which, I have all the time in the world for you.
We have a whole life before us.
Today's question is:
How can you be poor at disclosure
When you're a poet?

Fatima:

According to Ibn Manzur:
Disclosure is the appearance of a thing that has been concealed.

To disclose something is to make something appear, and the disclosure of something is its release.

Is that what poetry is?

Writing isn't a substitute for a friend who is a good listener, or for a psychologist, or a priest who hears confessions. If Ibn al-Mulawwah only recited poems to heal himself, let's remember, for the love of God, that the poems killed him.

Writing isn't a way to unload anxieties; it creates and intensifies them.

Writing is greater than life; it is the surpassing of it.

Writing isn't an allusion to a wound, it's the ongoing creation of one.

Writing is a spiral movement toward the horizon, not sitting for long periods on the psychiatrist's couch.

Writing is an act of listening more than one of disclosure, and is sometimes a *means* of listening. The text is formed, and the further you are from yourself, and wend your way toward the world that exists in you, the closer you are to being a poet.

Writing isn't curling up,
and it isn't spreading out.
It's a dance between the two.
I'm poor at disclosure,
but I write poetry.
I dance.

Isam:
Amen.

What can I do with you anyway, if you're fighting me the whole way? You impose your rules, dispense your existence into my mouth drop by drop like a drug . . .

Write your poetry, your unforgivable poetry.

Let it hang down like that, in your own way, over your heart.

Pour it out carefully,

Release it . . .

Like a stream that has rebelled against the river, and gone on singing the virtues of deviation.

Write your poetry, your dance, your femininity, your pain, your lament, and your song.

Write, Fatima, but . . .

Talk to me sometimes.

I'll sit here and wait.

By the way,

It was a captivating dance.

Fatima:

I sometimes imagine that I see the world chewing on its sleeve and running barefoot. On the sand, running barefoot.

When I see it running like that, I wonder: where are its sandals? Where did it lose them? Where did it forget them? Then I understand what's going on, what's really going on with the world: the world took off its sandals and ran away.

I am a sandal.

Isam:

I am hung up on you.

You are a seed growing in the heart.

I wait, every day, with each message, each word, each letter.

I wait for you to open up, for the time to come when you appear fully in my life, like Rilke's rose that, "petal against petal, rests within itself, inside."

I talked to my mother about you today. I told her I've met a girl who is actually a poem, and that we're writing to each other. I told her you're the only thing that can restore what I'm missing, that she has to stop writing girls' names down in the black book that she brings with her to all the weddings as if she's arranging my funeral, and that she should write your name only: Fatima.

My mother asked me many things. Did you meet her in the writers' group or at the university? What does she study? Does she wear the hijab? Is she tall or short? From the city or country? Shia or Sunni? Who are her parents and what is the name of their seventh neighbor? When I told her that I would find out those things in the next three years, given the unforgivable slowness in my ability to get to know you, she got up from the table thinking I was making fun of her.

My mother likes to put everything on the table from the start, to deal with the world "openly," as we say. She starts throwing this and tossing that and saves a few things . . . she's very pragmatic, unbearably practical. The only diagnosis I have for this illness is that she doesn't read poetry.

No one can read poetry and stay practical like that, searching for the direct advantage, making paintings and poems and songs all meaningless things because they have no 'use.' Like it or not, we have to admit that we live in a world that doesn't see beauty as a necessity.

My mother thinks that as long as there is no real material gain or some kind of recognition—something I have failed to achieve—I'm not good enough, and so the decision I made to study comparative literature isn't a 'logical' decision. Focus on the word 'logical' here. Does it make you smile? I hope so.

Let's return to my mother. My mother wants me to study accounting so I can get a government job, because the cost of living is always going up. One of her countless ways of terrorizing me is to force me to do poetry readings, saying, You have five more "shows" and if you don't receive sufficient acclaim, it would be foolish to pursue writing any further. I am a clown in a great circus called "Literature"! Speaking of poetry, my mother only acknowledges two poets, and only has room in her memory for them: al-Mutanabbi and Nizar Qabbani. She calls what I write "gibberish poetry." The prose poem is pure heresy, a blatant departure from the true faith, a type of literary apostasy, God forbid. A couple of days ago she called one of those hacks who writes 'light' poems and asked him to give me advice on writing the "correct" way. . . .

So, Fatima. Are you smiling now, like me?

Even so, I write without a grudge and with much gratefulness for what writing really is. I bring the crazy things I write to her so she can be the first one to read them, not because she loves what I write, but because it's my way of telling her I love her.

My mother and I are different in every way, we debate all day. She takes me shopping and asks me to try on a pair of pants. In the fitting room she waits for me outside, repeating, Okay, so what did we decide about your latest poem? Are you sure about the title you chose? "Regression"? I've never read a poem called "Regression." Listen, son, why don't you write a patriotic poem? There's an audience for those poems, as you know.

She's harsh and kind at the same time. Her harshness is affection, and she has a strong hunger to control everything. Her problem in this world is that poetry can't be controlled by anyone. I think she will like you a lot, Fatima, because you curl up into your-self like a secret. She'll think you've surrendered, and she'll say: this is a suitable daughter-in-law for me.

By the way, don't you dare say something about yourself, something awful like in your last message.

Only beautiful things can be compared to you.

I love you more than your miserable mind can imagine.

I love you, silly.

I love you.

Isam

Fatima:

Dear Isam,

I loved every line you wrote about your mother. It made me smile several times.

Perhaps if you practice more, you'll succeed in making me laugh.

I thought about telling you about my mother, to retrieve her from memory, before she latches onto a cloud and rises into the sky.

My mother is from Muharraq. My mother is a drop of honey on a fingertip, and everything flowing from her depths is blue. She looks like Bahrain, and the mermaids, and the gods of Dilmun.

In my childhood, on our many trips to Bahrain, the sky looked ample and close, "within arm's reach," as Darwish says. There were many seagulls, storks, and happy dreams.

Not a day goes by without me wondering, what am I doing here, far from my mother's country? The blue is scarce and the air dry.

Why did my mom's sister leave me in the care of my older brother? Why did she decide this is better for me? I don't really understand why, Isam.

Saqr takes me to visit my aunt once a year. We stay one day then come back. On my last visit I told her that I wished to stay with her. She said, "You always have a home here, but as you see, it's a small place. The boys have grown up, and you're a girl."

Enough about me. Let's return to my mother. My mother is very beautiful, and she makes exceptional trifle, making sure to put fruit in the Jell-O. She loves lace and pearls. Before she left, she protected me from the ugliness of the world, and after she passed, I started to see boils and pits and traps in the world's face.

When she wanted to wake me up, she'd gently crack my toes and fingers, and I'd wake up slowly. She helped me name my toys, she read me stories, and, because I asked, she covered the walls of my room with floral wallpaper that looked like wrapping paper, decorated with purple and violet flowers.

I don't like the color of my walls now—it's a wasteland of white.

I don't like that I have to go down fourteen steps to reach the place that is mine.

A terrible place.

Still, what I wish for most these days is for my brother to get arthritis in his knees, so he'll stop coming down those steps.

I am starving to touch the world outside. I am Rapunzel, and instead of a tower with a window I live in a windowless tomb. The computer screen is my window. Are you going to be my prince?

So, Isam, what have we learned from this lesson?

My parents are dead, my brother is a prison warden, and I miss Bahrain a lot.

It seems I've gotten better at disclosure.
Write me a lot, write me more.
Fatima

Isam:

I've been reciting the lines of al-Muthaqqib al-Abdi since yesterday. His Fatima makes him suffer wonderfully. I want to sit with him on the couch in the hall and sing: "O Fatima, before you go, give me some joy!"

Isam:

Fatima,

I want to see you.
The emptiness is great and my heart wails.
Come.

Fatima:

Since I met you, my heart is no longer mine.
I am far and you are near.
It seems we won't stop.

What you're asking for is a leap. The pit is deep and my legs are weak.

If I say no and stay like this, in your email inbox, me writing to you and you writing to me,

I would know that you'll be mine for the rest of my life.

But you want more.

You want to risk a lot for a little
Because a lot is a little
And a little is more.

I won't risk us.

I'm a coward and you are demanding.

Isam:

I no longer know what to say, Fatima.

I'm depleted.

I hug the pillow to my chest and go to you in my thoughts.

I'm rusted and hung up and broken
Like an old lantern.
The only thing that lights me up is you.
This writing has become agony.
Have mercy.

Fatima:

I read your letters, then I write them out by hand on colorful scraps of paper.

I fold the scraps into squares, tiny squares.

I hide them in glass jars,
They used to be jam jars, apricot, I think.

They prefer poetry to jam, and are happy with their new job.

The things you write bring me back to life,
Even though your suffering is killing me.

Talk to me about things, about colors, about scents and meanings.

I want to see the world through your eyes.

Open the door and go out now, tell me what you see.

My heart is open wide
As if a window.

Isam:

I left my room today. I did it for you. Even though my spirit, in one way or another, stayed in front of the computer screen, ill and foolish.

Can you feel me? I am gently taking hold of your hand as if I'm afraid it will break in my grasp, and

wrapping it around my arm. Like a European gentleman I open the door for you so I can walk with you.
Can you see the sea, Fatima? We'll go there, you and
I. We'll take off our shoes and throw our socks in the
air. Our feet will sink into the sand and our walk will
wander, then we'll go into the water. Can you feel the
water, Fatima? The sea is refreshing as it touches your
toes. I am jealous—you and the sea are infatuated
with each other, and I . . . I suffer through it, I fake a
smile, fail, I think I'll carry you between my arms until
I anger the sea. You won't like this, of course, and
the sea won't like it, but no matter. This world is not
designed entirely to please your moods. The sea has
no mood, damn you both.

I'm not joking, Fatima, I spent the whole day
walking with you on the beach. I was alone, and with
you. You were so real it made my muscles contract
and gave me goosebumps. Every few minutes I wondered, when will this miserable girl be with me?

I want to see you.
Even the sea wants to see you.

Tomorrow I'm going to stand in front of the entrance
of the college,
Stubborn as a mast.
I will look at you from afar.
You'll wave at me, if not with your hand then in
your heart.
That's my faintest hope and far less than I deserve.
The end.

Fatima:
Let's pretend—for the sake of argument or bluff—that
there's hope of some kind of meeting.

With a slap of the hands,
Contact that awakens the electricity in our veins.

Let's suppose—comically, hopefully—that a meeting like this
Isn't impossible,
That we can linger on the sidewalk without owning what we say,
That one of us can put their fingers
In the other's pocket,
Just to see.

Let's imagine that we could smile at each other
Without the veil over our emotions being breached,
Escape—in spite of it all—the whips of iniquity
As they carve into our backs a map of virtue.

Let's imagine
For a moment perhaps
That this thing that
Has drawn us to it
Isn't love

That the love that has drawn us
To it isn't a problem
That we never were

Isam:
I saw you today,
My angel,
Bright as a poem.
You're so beautiful.

Fatima:

My heart went crazy at the sight of you, off in the distance.

I'm shaking.

I wanted to wave to you,
But I felt I was doing that without moving.

I can feel you under my skin. How did you do that?

A Loaf of Bread and a Wooden Table

EVERY DAY THERE IS A poem. The poem grows leaves that are more poems. In each poem is a hundred poems, a hundred worlds, a hundred other places, invented time, countless homelands. There are skies, streets, sidewalks, and cafés. There are angels and madmen and vagabonds.

In poetry I put my hand in his and walk. In poetry he would brush his fingers through my hair and smooth its tangles. In poetry we'd meet and I felt less alone, and my wild heart grew gentler.

I don't think I've had a happy life, except for those days, the days of poems, the days of furtive email messages outside the cell's grasp. I was free and I was creating a world for myself. I made peace with things and learned, slowly, how to love, and how to be loved.

We were both twenty when we met, and love provided us with a language that gave us a place to stay, a strong roof over our heads, a loaf of bread, and a wooden table.

The stark whiteness of the outside world grew more remote, and I started—inside my poems—to build and furnish homes, filling them with paintings and music. I nested deep within poetry, and wondered: did I love him because of poetry? Or did I love poetry because of him? Is it possible for us to be anything outside the limits of language? Do we really exist, meat and bone and drops of blood, or are we both, for the other, made of paper?

What does he know about me?

Just my soul.

Is that enough?

Is love ever enough?

I felt the tree inside me growing foliage. Slowly I let go of my thick skin and the iron hooks that I hung on my shoulders so as not to forget the vicissitudes of the world and the inevitability of death.

I was letting go. Letting go of the wound, which was all I had been. I was making myself outside of it, I was being born again, and I was letting go of everything I'd endured, for the sake of my second birth. I was the one giving birth, the one being born and the one for whom I was born all at once. I was becoming free.

Three months passed.

Adam and Eve

Come to the university library tomorrow at ten, and have some good excuses ready in case you're late. I don't want to feel neglected.

WE MET SEVERAL TIMES, ISAM and I. We met at the university library, between the shelves of poetry and in the discussion rooms. We touched the covers of thick books, inhaled the scent of old dust, distilled wisdom, and pure genius. Our knees touched, our fingers too. We perished and were saved; we clung to poetry.

"Fatima, at last."

I smiled and turned away. He looked closely at me, drinking up my face. I felt nervous; he laughed softly.

"Do I frighten you?"

"A little."

He put his hand in his pocket and pulled it out again.

"I brought you something."

He set a doll on the table in front of me. It was wearing a lilac dress, and had magnets affixed to the back. It would look cute on the fridge, were that possible, if little dolls didn't chase away the angels in the republic of the big brother.

"You brought me a toy?"

"Do you like it?"

"It's lovely."

"I've been buying you a lot of things lately."

"Really? Like what?"

"A jump rope."

"You're joking."

"No."

"What else?"

"Crayons."

"I love crayons!"

"A highlighter."

"Nice!"

"Stuffed bunnies."

"What else?"

"When I go to a restaurant I order a meal for you and have it placed in front of the chair across from me. I have imaginary conversations with you. I pretend you're complaining there's too much garlic."

"You're crazy."

"True."

"Where are the rest of my toys?"

"In the car. I had to make sure you liked them."

"Ah. You took precautions."

"Kind of."

"I also frighten you, it seems."

"A little."

We smiled.

That's how we met. We met several times. Sometimes Hayat was there, sometimes she wasn't, sometimes poetry was there, sometimes it wasn't. We started the fire of questions, blew on the coals so they wouldn't go out. We burned our fingertips and our hearts, and entered the darkness, exhilarated by the absence of a map, the sudden disappearance of rules, and the gradual fading away of answers. We were going straight into the mysterious fog and discovering the world as if it had just been created, emerging fresh and hot from the oven. Things were no longer heavy with meaning or entangled in a long history of disappointment and defeat. We were the first man and the first woman, a book between us, the forbidden fruit of the tree of knowledge. The apple of temptation.

"Can we talk on your cell phone?"

"No."

"Why not?"

"Email is safer."

"What are you afraid of?"

"Of this."

"What's this?"

"Crazy."

"This is the most reasonable thing in the world."

"What we're doing isn't just a crime in my brother's eyes, it's a crime in everyone's eyes: that man sitting over there, the librarian, the Egyptian security guard, the mosquitoes."

"Look around you, Fatima. People have changed. They interact without any problems at all. Do you see? There? Male and female university students talking and drinking coffee together—it's completely normal."

When the world is made new and innocent again, everything becomes possible. Innocence alone can lead to mistakes. There among the library shelves it seemed like we were shedding the presence of time and the burden of place. I would rest my head for a long time against a shelf of books and follow Isam with my eyes while he took out a new volume of poetry from the shelf, opened it in the middle, and read standing up, taking great care to choose the "right poem," as he said. It wasn't so much that we always talked about poetry, as poetry's magic worked its way into everything: eyelashes, fingers, and unscrupulous dreams.

"What have you been writing lately?"

"Letters. Just letters."

"I love your letters."

"And I love yours."

For a moment perhaps, a very brief moment, something funny occurred to me. What if this was how things were with

Adam and Eve, when the senses were emerging from their innocence and tasting the world slowly, when language was being revealed like manna, making the rock a rock and the tree a tree, giving things weight and meaning as they crept slowly into existence through . . . language? Through a couple? Did love unfold like that, as though it were a flower to be discovered, like uncharted land, innocent and pure and green?

I asked myself, unconvinced: is he real, this poet? Is he real? He's a man, a strange man. He doesn't seem like a wolf. Can my brother be right and my heart wrong? My fingers feel comfortable between his, it seems like he wants to protect me, he's strong as a roof, spacious as a sky.

"Do you publish your writing?"

"On a blog."

"Really? And you're hiding this from me?"

"It's just random junk I put together. It's not nearly as good as I want it to be."

"You can't make that decision for me. What's your blog called?"

"Secret."

He searched for a blog called "Secret" and didn't find it. He has a lot of lines around his eyes that spread out across his forehead. He looks five years older than me even though he's just two. He's not tall or muscular, he doesn't look like the dark knight on the white horse, and this love that is slowly being woven between our fingers doesn't match my expectations or my fantasies or the Cinderella stories. It's greater.

"I wanted to ask you . . ."

"What?"

"Would you be opposed to joining a writers' group?"

"Are you kidding?"

"Not at all."

"You know that's not possible."

"We could figure things out."

"How?"

"There are morning groups, sponsored by the university. I'll try to arrange the time to match the breaks between your classes. Once a week, Fatima. What do you think?"

"I don't know."

"It would mean a lot to me, Fatima. I need you there. The silly discussions are unbearable and the writing that people submit . . . it's torture."

I laughed.

"I'm really counting on you to join."

"You're kidding, of course."

"I'm serious. I even thought about canceling the group. Then—then I thought, if you were with me there, we could take the discussion to a higher level. You and I are a team, Fatima."

"That's exciting!"

"It's more than exciting!"

One door leads to another, one window opens onto another. The heavens multiply and expand further and further. The walls come loose and the prison bars fall away. There are openings, and spaces, and margins for me to move around in. There's space enough to touch and experience the world. Life can still grow and bear fruit.

"I've been taking a lot of risks for you lately."

"That's to be expected. I'm worth it."

"Gladly I Race to My Death"

"How long have I known you?"

"Nine months."

"That went by fast."

He opened the door for me, motioned with his head.

"This way."

I trust him as much as I doubt myself. I acknowledged him and entered. We were in the student lounge where the writers' group he led was supposed to meet. He came in after me, rubbing his hands in excitement.

"Damn, I've waited a long time for this! I can hardly believe it!"

"We'll have to do something about your language."

"Sit down."

We sat down. Modern blue chairs, a low square table made of white glass. A transparent blue vase with yellow artificial flowers that had an IKEA price tag on them. Scattered books and shelves, a television screen showing the news, a Nescafé coffee machine, a carefully folded prayer rug in the corner.

"Are we early?"

"They're on their way." He sat to my right, then turned toward me and stared. Just like that. He looked at me as if I was something to look at. As if I were created for him to look at.

"What's wrong with you?"

"I'm looking at you."

"Why?"

"'Looking at a beautiful face is heaven.'"

"You're crazy."

"'Only those who have gone mad know the pleasure of life.'"

"'Life, as I see it, is a treasure, diminishing each night . . .'"

"That's okay. 'Life is nothing but suffering and struggle . . .'"

We laughed.

Lately we'd been talking in poetry. A man and a woman cannot be alone, with them always is poetry. Minutes later the others arrived, a small group of three men and three women who were talking and laughing together when they came in. They were acting with a naturalness that surprised me.

"Hello!"

No one disapproved of anything they saw. No one assumed anything bad.

"So you're Fatima?"

"Fatima! Finally we meet."

"Isam won't shut up about you. You're all he talks about."

"He gave us a real headache."

"'Fatima said . . . Fatima wrote . . .'"

"'Fatima can't come, Fatima agreed to come!'"

"'Fatima this, Fatima that . . .'"

Then, they all began quoting poetry:

"'O Fatima, were all the women in the world in one town and you alone in another, I would blindly follow you.'"

"'O Fatima, enough of this coquetry . . .'"

"'O Fatima, gladly I race to my death . . .'"

"'Appear, O Fatima, before death comes . . .'"

"'O Fatima, you know not the love in my heart nor the tears pouring from my eyes . . .'"

Isam scolded them. "I was trying to teach you something, you blabbermouths."

"No, you scared us."

"Sit down, just sit down. It's not enough to be late, you have to embarrass me in front of her too?"

I smiled, unable to believe it. They were very taken with being poets. I liked them immediately. They were filled with joy, had animated spirits. Like little bunnies, like bubbles.

The discussion began and words were flying everywhere. They expanded with their ideas. A voice rose and another rose over it. The discussion grew heated, and I sat silent, listening, my heart fluttering. There were seven people in this room talking about poetry, my personal definition of bliss.

What is poetry? What are words? Are they a way for us to understand each other or the cause of all misunderstanding? Are they a verbal reflection of things, a symbol signifying things that exist in the world, or are they a way of seeing the world? Are they merely a means for meaning or are they meaning itself? Are they part of the world or do they transcend it? And what about words that have contradictory meanings, conflicting ones, open to endless interpretation? How can something so loaded and packed with meaning be used as a means of communication, and what is the poet supposed to do with them? How can poetry reach us if it isn't a means of communication? Is poetry the end or the means?

"I want to hear what Fatima has to say," Isam said.

They went silent and turned toward me.

"About what?" I asked him nervously

"I want to hear from you. How do you deal with words that are concentrated, packed with meaning? How do you treat them in a poem? How do you bring them into submission?"

"I don't."

"What do you do then?"

I took a deep breath.

In the Beginning Was the Word

"WHEN I WORK WITH A WORD, any word, I feel its weight in my hands, in my heart, on the tip of my tongue. I taste its complex flavor and its temperament, which is more like a puzzle, and try to unleash its essential meaning.

"When I handle a word, I try to bring it joy and ignite its possibilities by putting it somewhere it loves, in a place that surprises and delights it.

"I always imagine that words grow sluggish and lifeless, that they get worn out and exhausted from overuse, and need to feel new and fresh, just born, emerging from the primordial fog into the world of meaning. On an adventure, like a mermaid in love.

"It's hard to mention a word in a text without becoming ensnared in its history. Can you, for example, use the word 'sky' without dragging along with you a long line of words? Without summoning a tribe of relatives, a gang of friends: high, clear, pure, blue, paradise, the divine.

"When you work with a word like 'sky,' you bring its long history of relationships with you, but is this what the word really says? Is this what it suggests to you? What about its familiar whisper in your heart? Does it make sense that the word would say the same thing to all of us?

"I think that what a word says to me is different from what it says to you, and if for you the sky is clear and blue and so on, to me it suggests other things entirely, like distance and impossibility. Thinking about the sky makes me feel like an orphan, and this emptiness that exists between the sky and the earth fills me with loneliness to my core. But that's just me. Let's return to the word 'sky.'

"You'll see that it has started to conjure up different types of words, or a new tribe of relatives, and to forge new relationships that animate it and make it clearer and more agile in the body of the poem. And when you realize that, you feel that you've become lighter and freer to play with this word, the word 'sky.' It has become possible for you to throw it into your poem without being entangled in its ancient history and linguistic customs, and isn't that your job as a poet?

"Let's take another word. Think about the word 'white.' What does this word do in a text, or what does a text do with it?

"White is perhaps the color of milk and motherly love, purity and virtue. It's the favored color of prophets, and it is also the color of knowledge and madness. We know that white is the origin of the seven colors, and that the rainbow is white stabbed by seven knives. White might be all this, but it is more. White is death, white is nonexistence.

"You, as a poet, must be terrified—or at least moved—by the oppressive whiteness of the page, you must feel its gleaming blank face with all the fear in your heart. It provokes your being.

"Now think about how these words balance against each other. White is madness, madness is purity. White is knowledge, knowledge is nonexistence. While pouring yourself a glass of milk early in the morning, you meet new relationships and chemical reactions that had never occurred to you.

"You cross over from poetry to philosophy from who knows where.

"What I'm trying to say is that words, like us, are burdened by their past, and they, like us, are freed of it through poetry."

"If the Boy Falls in Love?"

WE WALKED SLOWLY THROUGH THE corridor. We savored the
spring afternoon on our warm skin. I felt a tingling in my
head and a lightness in my feet, as though I were walking on
air. How beautiful life could suddenly become! I looked at
him out of the corner of my eye. He was like me, his head in
a poem and his feet on the ground.

We didn't need to speak. We walked for minutes as if
they were days, and during those minutes I wasn't anxious
about anything, as if I were immune to scandals. It didn't
bother me for the students to see us together, and it didn't
bother me that we were each smiling through the other's
mouth. It didn't bother me that the chemistry that drew us to
each other had started to diffuse and spread, drawing other
beings toward it. I felt secure like never before, as if poetry
was protecting me from harm, and Isam was poetry.

"You were amazing today."

I smiled happily. I also felt that what I'd said was nice, and
I saw them looking at me wide-eyed, in awe of my words. I
saw their fascination and felt unbelievably happy.

"I'm happy."

"You liked the meeting?"

"I loved every moment."

"You charmed them, Fatima."

"You exaggerate."

"Exaggerate? I was there and saw everything. I was on the verge of shouting in their faces: 'Back off! Get away! This girl is mine, I found her first!'"

I laughed deeply. I felt his steps slow; he was drunk from poetry. He leaned against the column to his left and looked at me. Again he looked at me.

"You know you're annoyingly beautiful?"

"Knock it off."

"Unforgivably?"

"Stop."

For a moment things shook and lost their serenity. I started looking around, afraid someone had heard us. Isam laughed, and commented wryly:

"The map folds up on itself."

"Don't be silly."

"Just tell me, since you are the map: 'If the boy falls in love, what is he to do?'"

I picked up where he left off: "'Hide his love and keep his secret. Obey everything and surrender.'"

"'And how is he supposed to hide it when the boy is being killed by love, and every day his heart breaks?'"

"'If he doesn't have the forbearance to keep his secret, nothing but death can help.'"

His smile widened sadly, and like someone on the verge of death he sang to me: "'I heard, I obeyed, then I died, so send my greetings to he who did to love forbid!'"

Real Conversation, Virtual World

"IT'S BEEN A YEAR."

"I can't believe it. A year went by that fast?"

"A year, Fatima! An entire candle!"

"We should celebrate."

"I want my present."

"Oh really?"

"I'm not kidding. I think I deserve a present. An 'annual bonus.'"

"What do you want?"

"More you."

"I was with you yesterday, in the writers' group!"

"I want something else. Actually, I already have it, I just need you to agree."

"What are you saying?"

"I signed you up for a morning poetry reading."

"Are you kidding?"

"Nope."

"Are you trying to kill me?"

"A year, Fatima. A whole year, and you don't trust me?"

"Are you crazy? What have you done?"

"I've taken care of everything. All you have to do is come. Your name won't appear in the announcement or on the posters or in the newspaper. There will be no press, no cameras. Nothing to be scared of. All you have to do is come, like every other time, at the same time. You'll sit to my right and read your poetry. Ten minutes, Fatima, just ten minutes!"

"Are you sure?"

"It's no different from the writers' group. You've been a member for three months and nothing bad has happened. Trust me."

"I don't know what to say."

"Say yes. My annual bonus."

"And if something happens?"

"I won't let anything happen. I'm not going to let you go so easily."

A Small Mistake

"WHAT ARE YOU SAYING?" ISAM shouted.

Nisrine was upset, nearly in tears.

"You promised me you'd take care of it yourself!" he said.

I entered the room. I didn't understand what was going on. I looked at them openmouthed. Nisrine was defending herself, her hands waving in the air.

"It was a mistake. There was a mix-up with the papers."

"Do you realize what you've done?"

Isam was clenching his teeth, hitting the table with his fist. The table shook and his hand nearly exploded. A wound on his hand. His ears turned very red. So that's how he looks when he's angry. I hadn't imagined him capable of that.

"What is it?" I asked stupidly. "Why are you shouting?"

My tone was critical. Sympathetic toward Nisrine, biased toward her before I even knew what the mistake was. He looked at me with eyes that were too shiny. Tears?

Isam was crying over me.

I gasped. "What's wrong with you?"

"Fatima, I'm sorry."

"About what?"

"There's been a mistake."

My heart sank deep inside me. I readied my senses for the disaster.

"A mistake?"

"Your name is listed in the reading announcement."

I swallowed. My legs felt weak and I sat on the edge of the chair, shaking. The end days had started and hell approached. I was done for. My blood filled with the feelings of the sacrificial victim before the knife. It was finally my turn. My mouth dry, my voice shaking, I asked, "How?"

"The papers got mixed up at the printers. They printed the old version."

"What am I going to do now?"

"Don't worry, Fatima."

He sat on my right and held my hand, squeezing my fingers. My fingers melted in his warmth. I lifted my eyes to him, at a loss.

"We'll take care of it," he swore to me.

I whispered, stunned, "He'll kill me."

"You're going to be okay."

"My big brother!"

"He won't find out about it."

"Impossible!"

A few minutes later the rest of the group entered, with cheerful, tired faces, out of breath.

"Everything is fine, guys!"

"What did you do?"

"We took all the posters and announcements down from the walls. There's no need to worry. Everything is under control."

They smiled.

"Really?"

"Everything is fine."

"You took down all the announcements?"

"Every last one! We tore them to shreds. We had a great time."

"And how will people find out about the reading?"

"By SMS. Don't worry."

"No one's going to come anyway."

"No one pays any attention to us."

With these guys everything turns into an entertaining story, something to laugh about. I looked at them disbelievingly. With as much gratitude as possible, I let out a deep breath and wiped my tears, looking at my friends, my love for them flowing from my eyes.

"Thank you."

"There's still one problem. One small problem."

Isam understood. His eyes boring into mine, his face serious like never before. I looked at his face and saw love.

"What is it?"

"The newspaper announcement. In tomorrow's edition, page sixteen. You'll have to get rid of it yourself."

"No problem."

We smiled.

Everything was fine.

Or so we thought.

Fatima:
Good morning, Isam.

Four hours until we meet. It's now 6:00 a.m., and I've been awake since 4:30 waiting for the paper to arrive, so I can tear up the announcement. So I can tear up my name.

I spent last night thinking. How many Fatima Abdel-Rahims are there in Kuwait? Hundreds, or thousands?

I felt like I was being too cautious. What are the chances that my name is the same as someone else's? What's the likelihood that Saqr will read the culture pages of the newspaper? The pages he has never read? Never will read? The pages for the misguided, for those who have gone astray, the intellectual deviants?

Still I said to myself: one must take precautions. I have a lot at stake if things go wrong.

I waited for an hour and a half, until the paper arrived. I picked it up with a trembling hand, a trembling heart. I opened it to page sixteen, searched for my name, and found it right away. I read it several times and felt so happy, Isam, I felt so happy and I filled my lungs with the morning air and said, Come, Mama! Look at your little girl!

My name is in the paper, Mama, in a list of poets! I was falling, Isam, into that eternal well that I told you about, into the bottomless pit of my orphanhood, that never ceases to be reborn and resurrected. Burning like a fresh wound. Why don't the pains die away, Isam?

I couldn't stop the impertinence of my thoughts, and the anger that rose from my chest into my ears, making them burn and redden (are you paying attention . . . ?).

If things had been different, right now we would be throwing a party. I would be dancing. But instead I am anxious, falling to pieces, tearing up the paper, the paper of my victory over orphanhood. I tore it up, Isam, I tore it up and left, as if I were tearing up something shameful.

My sadness is all-encompassing this morning, the morning of my first poetry reading. I feel that my life has been stolen, that this world isn't for me, and never will be.

I hope you've saved the announcement, the announcement with my name, and yours. I hope that you've shown it to your mother, that you celebrated with her, that you had a special breakfast for the occasion, pancakes for example, and coffee with milk for a change.

As for me, I will spend the next few hours reading "The Night Fatima Was Arrested." I will try to understand with Souad al-Sabah why I tore up the newspaper announcement with my name in it. Why did I tear it up, Isam? Why did I tear it up?

"This country circumcises women's poetry,
Wraps a noose around the sun when it rises,
To protect the safety of the family."

Things Shall Remain Between Us

"READY?"

Sometimes he has an ethereal smile like that, emanating from his face out of so much love. I say to myself that there's nobody like him. No one has this face so deeply advanced in love, lost in tenderness, stunned by the force of this love. A face sent from outside the world, as if it were a poem of flesh and paper, of ink and blood. With two charming dimples, a smile that goes to the furthest reaches of joy, and the light, all of the light, in the night of his eyes.

My heart rushed at me, as if it were beating in my ears. I heard its reverberations coming to me from a far-off place, a place deep inside me.

I took a deep breath and whispered, "Ready!"

"What are you going to read?"

"I haven't decided yet."

"Don't scare me, please. The 'force of nonexistence' and 'end of the world' and stuff like that has to remain between us."

"How possessive of you!"

We entered the room. The same room.

"Do you remember?"

"I remember."

The place where we'd met for the first time—before an impossibly beautiful year, like a dream fleeing the reality of place and rudeness of time. With the difference that today

I was sitting to his right, on a long wooden podium, to read poetry, my poetry. My poems, my little creatures, will wrap my voice around their shoulders and soar into the air. They will be liberated. I am setting them free today, weaning them, granting them their wider existence outside of me. Today was their independence day.

I was surprised by how many people there were. I whispered in his ear, "There are more than thirty people here!"

"Usually we have fifteen at most."

"Strange!"

"It's thanks to the announcement. Do you see the woman there, in the brown shirt?"

"Yes."

"That's my mother. She's here to check you out, so be nice."

"Are you serious?"

"Completely. She's my mother and she came because of you."

I lifted my eyes and quickly lowered them. She was looking at us with a knowing smile on her lips. Intelligence radiated from her face. A woman in her late forties, with milky skin, lines spreading out around her eyes, a small mouth, and keen glances. She made me nervous.

"She's beautiful."

"I know what you're getting at. Just say it: why didn't you inherit your mother's good looks, Isam?"

"Isam . . ."

"I had to say it."

"Have I thanked you enough?"

"For what?"

"For everything."

"You're happy?"

"Very happy."

"Then yes, you've thanked me enough."

The Poem Still in My Mouth

Everything is going as planned.
Everything is fine.
Everything except this heart leaping to the heights
  of fear.
Trembling before the intimation of the knife.

I SAID TO MY CRAZED heart: everything is going as planned. My turn will come and everything will be over. There's no need for your foolish bolting. You're overreacting.

My hands were sweating and my mouth went dry.

I am a sea, I am a desert.

My insides contracted, my fingers ached, and my skin crawled. I felt the rush of blood under my skin, and my heart, damn thing, flailing around in my extremities. I am a mad dancer.

A voice inside me cried: Get out of here, Fatima! Get out of here right now! I said to my heart: You're stupid and understand nothing! You want me to miss this moment because you are scared and cowardly! I'm telling you everything is going as planned but you don't believe it! You're so thick! My heart said, Run, Fatima. Run before it's too late.

I ignored my intuition and its divinations. I decided not to listen to the wailing inside me. I set the paper before me, the pen to its right. I took a breath from a far-off place and got ready to read.

I swallowed with difficulty. I was dry as a desert, drained and dehydrated. I said to myself: Everything will be fine when I put the poem in my mouth. The poem will replenish me, the poem will speak me.

Isam finished his last poem. They were clapping for him, and his mother smiled. He had done well. Nisrine came up to the podium. She was about to introduce me to the audience, to read my name in public, to announce my hour.

"A new face on the poetry scene in Kuwait . . . highly distinctive poems, transmitted through the intimacy of experience and her ability to grapple with existence . . ."

I heard the sound of Nisrine's voice, and another sound. A sound of steps approaching. Steps I knew. I knew their weight, I heard them every day, fourteen times, coming down to the basement, and going up to the world.

My heart is sad for you, Fatima.

Said my heart.

I heard the scraping of the shoes on the ceramic tiles, a sound that roused all of my instincts. I was the offering who knew the glimmer of the knife in the executioner's eyes. Everyone disappeared and the tomb was there. I was falling while the sound approached, and approached. The shadow reached inside. The face appeared from behind the door, the face/the inferno, the face/the gallows.

The face saw me and I saw it.

"The poet, Fatima Abdel-Rahim . . ."

I stood up, a string pulled taut. I was the bow and the arrow, I was the victim and the blood.

I gathered my papers. The mute whimper in my chest retreated, everything slipped from my hands, conspiring against me. The papers and the tears fell on the poems, on the ground, on my cheeks. The world disappeared into a drop of water. Everything was over.

I looked at Isam, from the twilight of water falling from my eyes. I wanted to say goodbye. Isam whispered uncertainly, Fatima, what's wrong? I didn't answer.

I looked at the face growing from this burning hellfire, at the valleys of scalding water in his eyes, the Zaqqum tree on his forehead. The whip and the cleaver and the iron bars and the menace in his furrowed eyebrows. I pointed at him and closed my eyes over my tears. I was a bird in the den of the beast, the sky out of wings' reach.

The hand that came down on my face, heavy as a bomb, burst my head against the wall, threw me to the ground.

"You idiot!"

Everything shook.

The world was yanked from its lovely frame.

"You dirty . . . !"

But I hadn't read a thing.

The poem was still in my mouth.

"You harlot!"

Isam ran. Saqr flung a chair at him, our friends jumped up, surrounded Isam. His mother threw herself on top of him. The voices came together in a single mass.

A blue light in my eyes, a red wailing in my head. I heard nothing but his voice . . . the voice of my beloved coming down from an eighth heaven. . . .

"He calls you by your name, you animal!"

My name must remain covered up. My name is a scandal.

His hand gripped my head, his hand was a pair of pliers, the pliers were dragging me . . .

To my immense confusion, gasping in pain.

"Get moving!"

But the poem was still in my mouth.

"You disgrace me, may God disgrace you!"

A second blow came down
From the heights of its might,
Landed on my face.

My poem ran from my mouth
A red thread.

Shoes

As if the sky were raining
Fingers, fingers

As if the hands were multiplying
On my cheek

Erupting from my face
Tearing it apart

Many things happened in an hour.

HE DRAGGED ME BY MY hijab along the length of the corridor from the room to the car. He shoved me into the back seat, pushed me in with his shoe. I curled up into a ball, I am a sin with tails. Some other things happened. He swore at me the entire way home. When the traffic light was red he'd take the black iqal off his head, turn around, and hit me with it. He stopped the car, pulled me by my arm. I dissolved in his hands, wet myself, collapsed. He lifted me by my arm, dragged me outside my poem, returned me to his grasp. The tomb opens its mouth.

He pushed me to the stairs, descending to the nightmare. He threw me on the bed, slapped me with his shoe. Raided my notebooks and pens, put them in a black plastic bag, and took them upstairs. He built a pyre in the courtyard. He burned García Márquez and Dostoevsky and Naguib Mahfouz, al-Mutanabbi and al-Maari, Mahmoud Darwish and Muzaffar al-Nawab. He sentenced them to death by fire on charges of heresy. My chest opened up to embrace my destruction. I am but fragments.

He came back panting, ashes dirtying his clothing, his hand, his forehead, and the tip of his nose. He circled the room twice, then headed toward the computer and yanked it from its place. He took the hard drive, the screen, and the cables that looked like arteries, the arteries extending from my heart to his. He took my only love story and left. Uprooted the tree inside me. I heard the sound of it falling. It was thunderous.

Again he came back, panting. He saw me huddled between the pillows, curled up into myself. I am a tear.

He pulled my hair: Where's the cell phone? I pointed to the bag. He opened it, dumped everything out, tore through its organs and limbs. He took my phone, the car key, my ID and driver's license, he took my life and left. Before he went upstairs, having fully completed his mission, he turned around one last time.

"From now on there will be no more university," he said. "You'll stay right here until the man who's willing to take you comes—God help you both."

I knew right away that the pain I was feeling was worse than any I'd experienced in my life. Not the pain of the blow, but the pain that came after—the horror of the eternal tomb and the vast empty desert of space, the horrible quiet that follows the storm. The destruction was complete and there was nothing ahead of me other than waiting forever for things that would never happen to happen. I would remain in a bubble of absence for three long years, decaying in the belly of the dragon, alone and confused and half crazy.

It was as if the whole thing were happening all over again: being orphaned, the tomb. The serpent of pain sheds its old skin and returns to life, with a wound that stings and burns even more. On that night, I curled up into a ball and whispered the only words I'd hoped to say before the disaster struck: Goodbye, Isam. Crying is a long road I walk barefoot.

Before me were many cells. Every day was a cell. Every cell led to another. The future? A figment of the human mind. From the place where I was curled up in a ball, like a dying baby chick, I knew that the future was merely "a boot stamping on a human face—forever."

In the beginning I resisted. I snuck outside the tomb and hid in Wadha's room. With trembling fingers I pushed the buttons on the phone and waited. A voice burst out: Dad! Hurry!

Fatima is calling her boyfriend! My aunt's voice came out of the receiver: Hello? Saqr rushed at me. Hello? He pulled me by my hair. Hello? He dragged me downstairs, always downstairs. Hello? I went down fourteen steps, beneath the line of consciousness. I live there. Hello?

After that attempt he started to lock the door. They'd open it for me when it was time to eat. That went on for months. After he got lazy and relaxed his grip, I didn't come out. I never made that phone call.

Relatives? I sat in their company like a marble statue. I was plucked from my tomb like plants are pulled from the ground. No one looked at me. I was nothing.

I see more than I can handle, more than is reasonable. The nail protruding from the table leg—I see it planted in my waist. The cracks in the wall—I see them in my chest, I see its whiteness in my eyes. I see my skin cracking like the paint on the wooden door. The world falls to pieces and collapses. Where are you, Isam? I am sick, my chest is bare, and my heart defenseless! Come smuggle me out of here, like something prohibited, like wine and marijuana and love. Come save me.

I have to die. Stamp out my senses bolting from so much fright. I have no window and there's not enough air. There is no sense in fighting, every struggle is a prolongation of the torture session called my life. In the end I will die, so why not now?

I search for scissors, a knife, a pen. Anything to sink into my wrist so I can flow outside of myself, slowly. Everything is far away. Saqr comes down to the basement every two or three hours, monitoring the progress of my ruin. He sees me sobbing and circling my cage like an animal, feels reassured, and goes back up. How can I die under surveillance?

I want to kill my sense of myself, to bury everything I am, to forget, to get very old, to get very old and forget. To empty my memory of myself, to peel my reality off like a skin, to peel off love and writing and everything in between, everything that might possibly send me back there, where my head burst against the wall and the poem ran red from my mouth.

I dream of love and poetry. I see Isam placing his fingers on my face, on my cracked skin, searching for me underneath. His face is everywhere, eating me from inside. His questions shatter my spirit: do your ears get red when you're angry? Just how much can a poet love you, Fatima?

I close my eyes, I summon his face, I see him suffering, reeling from so much loss, his voice pierces my head, he calls me . . . O Fatima, before you leave, before you die, before you're buried alive! Kiss me, love me, destroy me! I sit on the edge of his bed, I take his hand, I feel the fever rising from his body and passing into mine. I smile at him, I smile at him all sadness. I say goodbye, goodbye, my love, I will betray you in the worst way, I will forget you.

At the dinner table, day nine and a half.

Where's Fatima? Saqr asked. Badriya told him that they'd opened the door and I hadn't come up, then they'd called to me and I didn't answer. He went down the steps panting, spittle flying everywhere. He yanked the blanket off my body and pinched my forearm. Still pretending to be asleep? He pulled me upstairs by my hair, the bright light hurting my eyes. He sat me down opposite him. I saw him eating and heard him raving: You see what you make me do!

The spittle flew from his lips and landed on my face. First thing we see of you is this face? You'd rather die than sit with us? Or did you study French and write a couple of poems and now you think you're better than everyone else?

He waved a chicken leg in my face and continued: From now on there's going to be rules. The world isn't at your beck and call! I never laid a hand on you and now I'm the one who gets slapped in the face. You understand? I shook my head. Why aren't you eating? I don't want to eat. I want to die of hunger. He grabbed my cheeks with his oily hand, the smell of grease burning my nose. He squeezed my face until I opened my mouth, and forced rice inside, shouting: Eat, God damn you! Eat!

I was circling the bed and stepped on a piece of paper. The crackling under my feet gave me goosebumps. I'd missed hearing that sound. Any sound. I started tapping my fingers, throwing things, and discovered that I could talk, that I could use my own voice, and talk to it.

I talked to myself. I argued with myself. I laughed with myself, me and my face in the mirror, I am the evil witch and I am the one eating the apple. The things around me talk too. The crack, the roach, the keyhole. The chattiest, and rudest, is the Mitsubishi air conditioner. She examines me and laughs.

"What are you laughing at?" I ask.

At how crazy you are.

She laughs more; I hurl a box of tissues at her. "Next time it will be a shoe, Mitsubishi."

Susu, please.

"Susu?"

Yes, Susu.

"That's a name for a dancer in a cabaret."

She laughs. I threaten her. "From here on out there are going to be rules!"

Oh yeah?

"I make the rules here!"

Since when?

Another shoe at Susu's cheek. Bad Susu, Susu with the rotten teeth, Susu who swallows nails, Susu the oblivious. Ill-mannered Susu, no one loves her because she drools and makes the walls crack.

"You're such a bad girl! Bad and ugly! No one loves you! No one wants to see you! I'm going to lock you in the basement!

I'm going to hit you with a shoe! I'm going to burn your notebooks and destroy your things! You won't see the street or the sky or the birds until the idiot who agrees to marry you comes, God help you both."

What had to be done was done. They straightened me out. I am an obedient and compliant girl, capable of being brought into submission. I go upstairs. I sit on the chair. I open my mouth. I eat a couple of bites. I waste away. I disappear. I am an illusion.

I sit with them in the evening as they watch television and I stare into the mouth of nonexistence on the wall. I am a perfect corpse and I excel at my death like a star player. There is no longer anything requiring anyone's intervention or comment or objection. I am nothing. The system has won.

Finally I knew what it was that I had to do to please the big brother. I had to empty my heart of my heart. Kill the poem inside me. Return to the empty space that was before the big bang, to nothingness. Nothingness is the best that can happen to you. Nothingness is the shortest road to paradise. The life of nothingness is a life without sins. The absence of sin is right. The absence of life is right. I am a creature of nothingness. I perform my duties perfectly. I eat, I remain silent, I stare, I remain silent, I remain silent. What you do doesn't matter when it comes to a life of nothingness. What matters is what you don't do, a list of forbidden fruit that goes on forever. What matters is that you don't do something, not that you do. I no longer do things, and the things that I do are few and not harmful, like breathing, peeling the chipped paint from the door, sitting in the chair, chewing, swallowing, washing my hands, looking at the wall.

I don't wait for orders. There's no longer any need to beat me with a whip. I am a perfect creature performing its role in this "non-life" as perfectly as possible. I am the bird enamored of its cage, the one with a phobia of the sky.

*

There's a blue ink pen in my bottom drawer. How did this vagabond survive the pyre? The sight of it disturbed me so much I closed the drawer and jumped onto my bed.

There's a pen in my drawer, and I have plenty of walls for writing. What was I going to do? Would I write? What would I do with the pain if it returned? What would I do with writing? Writing is an act of remembering—what would I do with memory? Memory is an act of love—what would I do with love, what would I do with Isam? This little pen is capable of destroying everything, it disrupts the system that we, the big brother and I, created to keep my death coherent. This pen is a danger to me.

I thought for a few seconds then made up my mind. I opened the drawer, took out the pen. I broke it in my hands and threw it in the garbage. Susu laughed: Look at yourself, trembling over a pen! If you're that afraid of a pen, how do you feel about the air-conditioning vents?

"They disgust me."

Susu laughed. "What a faker you are, Fashila, you failure. The only thing you can do is talk. In fact, the last thing you want is for me to leave you by yourself."

"I'd prefer the company of ghosts to yours."

The broken pen lifted its head and asked me: Then why did you kill me? Its blood ran over my fingers, blue and very bourgeois.

Six months went by, and then time lost meaning and I stopped counting. Consciousness is shaped by time. No time, then, no consciousness, and hence, no pain.

The notebook of poems that I hid under the carpet—Saqr hadn't found them and didn't burn them. I had to do it myself. Rip out the pages poem by poem. My poetry is a bare tree, my hand is autumn, everything is in the process of falling thunderously nowhere. I outdid myself torturing

183

myself, more than the big brother had dreamed of doing. I told him, Give me the whip, I'll take care of it. I will beat my heart until everything inside comes out: love, poetry, and everything in between.

My bony yellow hand reached out for a poem a day. Without reading it a last time, I would start to fold it several times, my skillful fingers mechanically transforming it into a paper boat. I filled the laundry bucket with water and put the boat on its surface. I lay down on my right side and waited, with great forbearance, for the boat to grow heavier, for the paper to soak up the water, for the ink to dissolve and the boat to sink to the bottom of the bucket, for the poem to finish its slow, poetic, beautiful death, to drown in a bucketful of tears and meet its final end. The end of its suffering, estrangement, and beauty.

My poems drowned. I saw them crying and calling for help, and I didn't save them. I saw them waving their hands and swallowing water, breathing it in, dissolving in it. I killed my poems, while lying stretched out on my right side, pondering the process of drowning them like someone waiting for their socks to dry on a clothesline.

I killed my poems and walked in their funeral procession. I prayed for them and asked God to make them more worthy beings in future births. Both a gun and a knife cut flesh.

The prison mate got sick. She started looking at me victoriously and informing me that she was going to die, that she was going to leave me alone in the tomb and go to a better place. She started making a strange clicking sound, drooled on the wall more than usual, could no longer rotate her head, and started blowing hot, foul-smelling air in my face.

The place sank into a suffocating humidity, and I lay down on my right side watching her last pangs of death. You respectable old spinster, Mitsubishi, where do you think you're going? The world is an awful place. Stay here with me. I'll clean you more. I'll wipe the dust from you and take care of you, okay?

Saqr came down to the basement on a patrol, circled the place, and stopped in front of her. They exchanged meaningful glances, Susu and Saqr. He informed her that he was going to replace her with another. This old woman, fifteen years old, it's surprising she lasted this long. That's what he said. Saqr rarely praises anyone. No doubt Susu was proud of herself, despite her battle with death. She died content.

"Saqr has arthritis," the maid said.

That took long enough.

"Saqr started taking shots for diabetes."

This last news was devoid of meaning.

I saw Isam, tugging on my shirt, shaking me until I woke up.

Fatima! Fatima! It was Badriya. *Badriya?* She was shaking my shoulder. I pushed her. Fatima, wake up! Was it a dream?

"Do you usually sleep until afternoon?"

Time has no meaning when you're kept in a bubble of nothingness, to sleep in the morning and eat breakfast at night. The system is just a pretense. Did something happen? I want to talk to you about something. I couldn't look at her face—a blotch of white light had erased the right side of it.

"Did someone die?"

"No."

"What is it then?"

"How are you?"

"Fine."

A person without desire is a free person, a dead person, a person protected from disappointment and betrayal and pain. I am fine.

"What do you want?"

"I have nothing to do with this, Fatima."

"With what?"

"Everything. How Saqr treated you, preventing you from going to school. I tried to convince him to let you go back to the university. I just want you to know that I don't agree with what happened to you, but when it comes to you it's out of my hands. You know Saqr and . . ."

"Is that what you wanted to say?"

"No."

She got up and walked around the room, then turned toward me, an idea shining in her eyes.

"I wanted to tell you that I have a way for you to get out of here."

"I don't want a room on the second floor."

"That's not what I mean. I mean get out of your brother's house for good, to have your own house, Fatima. Do you want that?"

Leave the tomb? How? Who cares what's outside anyway, when the whole world is here? How would I give up my death that I'd worked so hard to achieve? How would I leave the tomb, when my limbs were scattered throughout the place, how could I leave the nail jutting out from the table leg and the broken drawer? And Susu with the rotten teeth, what about her? Everything in front of me was trembling in fear, saying, Don't leave us.

"What's wrong? Don't you want that?"

"I don't know."

Susu whispered, "You don't want anything."

"Fatima, are you okay?"

"Everything is fine."

"Are you going to give me an answer?"

"To what?"

"I've found you a husband, Fatima! Do you hear what I'm saying?"

Street Cat

This Must Be What Happened

FARIS CAME HOME AT EXACTLY four, because that's what he does every afternoon. If he doesn't come home at four, it means he's been run over in the street or is lying in a hospital bed. He comes home at 4 p.m. every day. The door creaks in his hands and he calls out to me, every day. When I don't answer he assumes—naturally—that I am in the bathroom, buried in bubbles.

He definitely opened the door and found the bathroom empty, the Jacuzzi dry. He probably thought I was in the study, because recently, very recently, I'd started to write. The bad habit he'd hoped I'd break. He'd look for me there and not find me. Then he'd go look for me in the kitchen. He'd say, Maybe she's making salad. I wasn't there either.

He would return to our bedroom and sit on the bed, surprised. He'd fail several times to get control of his thoughts, which were racing around the room, but then, in that spot where he sat on our double bed with the earth-colored bedspread decorated with goatskin pillows—pillows he loves and I hate—he'd notice that paper, a yellow Post-it stuck to the mirror. At that moment he'd encounter the letter informing him that I'd left.

He'd read it and not understand a thing, because it was incomprehensible. He'd take his cell phone out of his right pocket and call me, and when the phone company told him the number was out of service, he'd start to believe. His lips would part, despite the dryness and late afternoon thirst, and he'd whisper to himself, "She's crazy!"

Then his photographic memory would begin to discover the things that had disappeared: my comb, the Chanel eyeliner, and the bottle of oud essence. In the bathroom he'd notice the disappearance of my toothbrush and the Close-Up toothpaste. He'd notice that I left the Signal 2 toothpaste for him and he'd believe it a bit more, because he knows that I prefer the taste of Close-Up.

Most likely, different thoughts would hit him all at once. He'd have one idea and an idea that refuted it at the same time. He'd think in opposites and wouldn't notice his ideas contradicted each other. And because he wouldn't have the slightest idea what he should do, he'd most likely call Saqr. He'd dial his number then hang up before it rang. He'd say, The last thing Fatima would want is her childhood jailer. And he would be right.

He'd think that he should go to the police and submit a missing-person report—after waiting twenty-four hours. In this case he'd have to hide my silly goodbye letter stuck to the mirror and act as though I'd been kidnapped by a gang, and it would look as silly as in the movies. The policemen would start asking irrational questions: Does your wife have a secret lover? It would be embarrassing. But he had to do something, because his wife—a woman addicted to pills and to crying for long spells at night—had run away.

At first he would decide to go to the police to submit the report, then he'd notice a small, trifling detail that would enter his heart like a bullet. On the dinner table he'd find a spread of his favorite dishes: mashbous laham with truffles; arugula salad with haloumi cheese, sun-dried tomatoes, and toasted pine nuts; fresh orange juice; and lemon custard. The meal Faris dreams of having every day of his life until the world ends.

The gesture will shake him. Despite the anger, confusion, and heaps of incomprehension, it will touch his heart. He'll go out. He'll start the car and rest his head on the wheel. Here, most likely, he'll decide that he's going to wait. What is he going to wait for? He doesn't know. He will just wait. For his life to move from this moment to the one after it.

Because he can't stay at home he'll spend his night looking in every possible place. He'll start at the hospitals, to reassure himself that I'm not lying in an intensive-care unit, and then he will go to the cafés and restaurants we used to frequent together, and then to the sea. He'll search all of Kuwait and won't find me.

He'll go to every hotel he knows, the ones everyone knows. He won't notice this cheap three-star hotel, old and run-down. An unseen building—he'll walk right by it and won't see it.

Yellow Post-it

Dear Faris,

I think we did what we could, but it wasn't enough.
I'm too different, and it's more than you can bear.
Your love hurts me; my inability to carry on hurts you.
Recently my memories have started to afflict me, and
I've started to understand the extent of the damage.
I'm broken and unable to be in a relationship. I can't
be anything to anyone. Forgive me. And divorce me.
If you truly asked your heart, it would tell you that
my leaving is the best thing that could happen to you.

Take care of yourself,

Fatima

Had the paper been a bit bigger, I might have added other
things.

Apologies and more apologies. An insistent and bother-
some recall of the fits of fright in the night and my inexcusable
typhoons of anger. The antidepressants, migraine drugs, and
other indications of my misery and unsuitability. I probably
would have reminded him of how many times he found me
curled up in a ball on the bathroom floor, and how many times
he had to carry me to bed because I had decided to stop exist-
ing. I would remind him of the six sessions with Dr. Heba
Rushdi and her failure to pull me out of my eternal sinking
into scream. I would remind him of those days when I started

to stagger and rave, pointing at him and repeating al-Nawab's lines: "Filthy! We're filthy! No one is exempt." The news reports, the newspapers, the law, and even the touch of a hand and look in an eye. Everything disgusted me, as though I were an inflamed wound opening its eternal mouth to the world.

The poems by Muzaffar al-Nawab that tore through me, my long sobs. His arms when they encircled my body while he asked me to hold myself together and I . . . didn't hold myself together. I fell to pieces, collapsed. What do you want from me? I'd ask him. I want you, he'd say. I also want me, I'd say to him. Divorce me so I can have me. I won't divorce you, he'd say. I love you. I'd ask him, What do you—you—know about love? I'd raise my finger in his face and whisper al-Nawab to him: "Now I'll expose all of you." *There is no power and strength save in God*, he'd mutter. He'd dry my tears, carry me to the bed, call the doctor. Take her to the hospital, she'd say. Another injection, and another and another. He'd say, What do you want? I'd say to him, I want me for me, I want to write. He'd say, I can't do it! I'd say to him, I can do it. So why can't you let me do it? He'd say, You're my wife. Another injection in my vein. Waiting for another fit. And the one that follows, and the one after that . . .

Had the paper been bigger I might have reminded him of things he knows, that I am barren and can't give him sons, daughters, a future. That I'm happy being infertile and dance around repeating, "I'm barren! I'm barren!" That I nearly lose my mind when I imagine what would have happened if I'd brought a female into this world. Another female. A functional being to justify violation, a being cut into and undergoing revision, objectified, crucified, an offering to attract man's violence, to release the lust for blood. I used to squeeze my legs together in bed shouting at him so he wouldn't come near me. "It would be a disaster! A disaster!" I don't want to be the cause for another being brought into this frightening place, I don't want to be responsible for anyone's pain! I hugged the medical certificate that proved my infertility with more than relief. I hugged it and danced with it like a triumph.

Had the paper been bigger I might have told him that everything he does and every gesture he makes wounds me and causes me pain in a way he can't understand. I would have told him that I am worn out and wasted and interpret every glance of tenderness with the worst possible intentions. I would have reminded him that our life turned into a hell after I started writing again. That I can't not write because I tried not to write. That since I started resisting writing and denying its calls, language started biting my fingers and making them bleed. That I am lame and run into windows. I see witches in the mirrors and red apples and forests filled with spirits, and these creatures, these many creatures that chase me, won't leave me alone. I would have told him that I ran into Susu, even though I was sweeping the parquet floor in my super-deluxe apartment. I saw her there, on the wall. Her teeth were still rotten and she laughed at me and called me "Fashila." That I can't. I can't be in the same place as Susu. It's me or her.

Had the paper been bigger I would have told him about that night I dreamt of all the poems I drowned in a bucketful of tears. The poems assumed their old form and emerged— despite their complaints and dissatisfaction—from the fleet of ships that sank at the bottom of my sadness; the poems came back and filled me with memory. That morning I jumped out of my bed and opened my notebook and wrote, I wrote the memory that returned, I wrote it with rumpled hair without getting dressed and without washing my face. I wrote the return of language. I wrote until I ran out of strength and he returned at 4 p.m. to find me a near-corpse, wide-eyed at the horror of the past. Memory had ambushed me and torpedoed the mounds of delusion that I had tried to build up inside me in order to make this marriage succeed. The past had led a ferocious attack on me and laid everything to waste.

I would have told him many things had the paper been bigger, had my mind been clear as it is now, as I lie in my double bed, a double bed for one, for my loneliness and my running and my fits of fright. But I didn't. I wrote my paltry excuses on a yellow Post-it, stuck it to the bedroom mirror, and ran.

First Phone Call

ONCE IT WAS AFTER ELEVEN, I went out. I motioned to the employee at reception and he smiled. It was the beginning of winter, and I could get by with my cotton shirt and the scarf over my shoulders. The sidewalks were filthy and empty. In front of me was a gravel square and a parking lot. I walked next to the hotel, crossed the narrow alley between the hotel and the adjacent building. I walked until I reached a flower shop. I entered, said hello to the Filipina employee, and told her I'd lost my phone and needed to make a personal call. She pushed the phone toward me and went about her business. His voice came through to me on the first ring.

"Hello? Hello . . . ? Fatima? Is that you?"

"It's me."

"Where are you calling from?"

"Doesn't matter."

"You're in Salmiya!"

"Yes."

"Where were you all night?"

"Everything is fine."

"You're crazy! What were you thinking, leaving like that?"

"I . . ."

"You what?"

"I'm doing what feels right."

"You can't behave like this. You have no right to behave like this."

"Are we going to fight?"

"What did you expect? For me to plead with you?"

"I have the right to do what feels right. Actually, it's a crime not to."

"What about other people's rights? What about my right to be respected by my wife and for her to answer my calls and not run away from my home when I work like a dog to provide for her?"

I let out a deep breath. "Divorce me and this will all be over."

"No. Everyone is worried about you."

"Who?"

"All of us."

"Saqr?"

"Saqr is worried too. He's out looking for you in the streets."

"Liar."

"How long do you think I can cover up your recklessness?"

"Do you think I'm still thirteen years old and afraid of making him angry?"

"What are you planning on doing?"

"I'm figuring that out."

"What happened to your old number?"

"I got rid of it. Did you read my letter?"

"I read your stupid letter."

"I'm not coming back."

"I can't talk about our problem like this. Tell me where you are. We can sit down in a café and discuss things. Everything can be fixed."

I inhaled. Was I crying or laughing?

"What's wrong with you? Are you laughing?"

"I can't be fixed."

"Where are you? I'm coming to Salmiya. We have to meet."

"Did you sleep yesterday?"

"I haven't been back home since yesterday evening."

"You need to sleep."

"We need to meet."

"No."

"Why did you call then?"

"To tell you to divorce me."

"No."

"I'm going to hang up."

"Don't you dare!"

"I'll call you in a few days, after you've had a chance to think."

"Wait! Did you take your medicine?"

"Goodbye."

Because My Graves Are Many

I walked to Salim al-Mubarak Street, adjacent to al-Fanar Mall, al-Bustan Mall, and Layla Gallery Mall. I looked at the hotel in the Omniya Shopping Center, which looked nicer than my hotel. Maybe I would move here later. I had to do something about the mirror pointed in my face like an accusing finger.

I walked until I reached Maryam Shopping Center, went down to the basement level, and sat on one of the store couches, looking at the children's clothes and acting as if everything around me existed to give me a kind of solace. I looked at some frilly skirts, size one year and a half. I walked far in memory, went deeper. I returned to myself at nineteen, the first time I tried to run away. It seemed I was just finishing the job.

My little graves are all over the place now. I fall apart, and my pieces bury each other. I have unseen limbs and organs interred in public gardens and beaches and abandoned flowerpots. My graves are many, more than my parts and the days of my life, and much more than my body.

I was systematically buried alive, and when I pulled myself out of the pit and left I discovered that I was no longer capable of happiness. I had been emptied of my capacity to love and give and live. They drained me of my femininity. I was nothing.

"How much is this?" I asked the worker busy folding small pairs of jeans.

"Seventy dinars."

"I'll take it."

I needed to buy it. Even though my resources were barely enough, even though it was expensive, even though I'm not the mother of an eighteen-month-old child, even though I don't know anyone to whom I could give this pink frilly skirt. I needed to allow beautiful things into my life.

I took the small bag, with the skirt that I was much too old for, and made my way to the sea. I was going to spend the remaining hours of my day there. A free woman without attachments, discovering herself. I will commune with God. I will pray my prayer.

O Almighty, give me strength.
The strength to think, the strength of instinct,
The strength of the truth, the truth of the question.
The strength of the 't'
The flexibility of the 'e'
The lightness of the 'k,' despite the restraints
And the wrists tied together overhead.
O Almighty, give me strength!
The strength of the plant that cuts into the wall,
The strength of the drop that bores holes in the rock,
The strength of the prayer that brings rain.

Second Phone Call

FROM A PUBLIC PHONE BOOTH in the capital, in the enormous Ministries Complex building:

"Hello, Faris?"

"You're in Dayra!"

"Yes."

"Where?"

"Doesn't matter."

"You left me waiting a long time."

"I wanted to give you time to think."

"When's this crisis going to be over so you can come back?"

"I'm not coming back."

"Be reasonable. Don't cause a scandal."

"I'm not afraid of scandals."

"What are you afraid of?"

"Coming back."

"All of our problems can be solved."

"You won't divorce me?"

"I want to meet."

"No."

"Wherever you want."

"No."

"I won't touch you. I won't force you to do anything. We'll just talk."

"No."

"I can't discuss my marital problems while you're talking to me from a flower shop."

"I can't. It's not possible."

"I'm not going to divorce you over the phone."

"Does that mean you'll divorce me in person?"

"If I'm convinced that divorce is the solution."

"I don't want to see you. I can't."

"Then call from a private number. We can't talk about anything this way. I'm very worried. I can't sleep or work or tell anyone what is happening. You owe me this at least."

"Fine."

"I'll wait for you."

Hayat

"I COULDN'T BELIEVE IT WHEN you called."

She pulled her chair forward and hugged the paper coffee cup in her hands, using it to warm herself without seeming interested in its contents.

"After all these years!"

I still couldn't talk. I needed long hours just to look at her, at my childhood friend that I hadn't seen in four years. Her body had filled out a bit. She seemed comfortable in her white cotton shirt and black overcoat. Something in that face said it was her. Something, something else, said that she was much, much more.

It was silent. I couldn't move, and I didn't dare look her in the eye. I tried to fix my gaze on the sea outside. My hand grew stiff. My coffee got cold.

"I often wondered what happened to you after the reading."

Ah, the reading. A cloud in my head. The darkness of absence. A poem running from my mouth. Twilight. Facing the destruction of the world with a poem in my heart and a flower in my hand. Utter absurdity. I almost laughed! I tried to pull the bounds of the conversation outside the geography of my ruin. I was aiming for simpler and fewer things, a trivial and superficial conversation about the beauty of the sea and the cold weather. I tried to keep the conversation ordinary.

"How are you?"

"Um . . . how are *you*?" She squeezed my fingers. Her hand was warm. Her eyes kept boring into me.

"What did they do to you?"

"Solitary confinement, pretty much."

"For four years?"

"Three."

"I called you many times. Your old number was out of service. Then I got up the nerve to call your house. I called several times and your niece told me you were fine and didn't want to talk to me. I didn't believe her, and I didn't know what to do. I tried to visit you at home once. Without even opening the door, the maid informed me that you had gone abroad. I believed her because I wanted to. I imagined that you had gone to your aunt's in Bahrain . . ."

"I was just in the basement."

"How did you get here?"

"What do you mean?"

"How is it that now, suddenly, you can meet me in a café? When did that become possible?"

"Actually, I could have done that for a while. I mean, as far as being able to, not as far as being capable of doing it."

"Why?"

"I don't know. I think I felt ashamed."

She squeezed my hand harder, drinking me up with her eyes.

"Ashamed of what?"

"Of everything. Of the poem. Of the slap. Of being locked up. Of the marriage."

"Marriage?"

"Yes."

"Since when?"

"A year . . ."

"Congratulations!"

"For what?"

"Things didn't improve?"

"A little."

We replaced the cracked wall with wallpaper. I have a living room with modern furniture and cheerful colors in various shades of beige, pistachio, and olive green. A twenty-two-inch TV, three shelves for my books, movies. I have a multicolored Indian bedspread with golden threads. I have a doorknob that isn't broken. Windows. A vase filled with bamboo stalks, a beautiful Jacuzzi. Yes, things improved.

"Things improved a little, but I'm not okay."

"What do you mean?"

"I mean that I am not capable of living."

Her grip on my fingers tightened.

"I'm glad you called."

I tried to smile.

"What are you doing now?" she asked again. "Did you go back to school? Do you work somewhere?"

"Actually, I was . . . I was hoping you'd help me with this."

"With what?"

"Finding a job. I'm almost broke."

Her gaze shifted to the right. "I'll see what I can do. I know some people."

"Thank you."

"Have you thought of going back to school?"

"Maybe."

"You don't want to?"

"I'm not sure what I want. I'm not sure I even want to live."

"Does this mean you want to die?"

"I want to forget. Imagine taking your memory, haunted by all that destruction, to your new life. That wouldn't be nice."

"Have you thought that you might need help from a professional?"

"I've already done that. I have my medications."

"What medications?"

"Alprazolam."

"An antidepressant?"

"Yes."

"Are you taking it under a doctor's supervision?"

"I was in the beginning, yes."

"Then?"

"Then there were side effects that interfered with the treatment, so I started buying them illegally online, from a Korean dealer who sells prescription drugs."

I laughed. Hayat didn't.

"You shouldn't . . ."

I smiled. "After all these years you're going to try to protect me?"

"I've tried to protect you my entire life. I was even hard on you sometimes. That day when Saqr came into the room and slammed your head against the wall, I felt the whole thing was my fault. I pushed you."

"Did he really slam my head against the wall?"

"Have you forgiven me, Fatima?"

"Don't be stupid."

I saw tears in her eyes. I saw a half-smile on my mouth. I saw my old hurt nested in her depths. I saw the pain spread while I watched, while I watched with a half-smile on my lips. She dried her tears with the edge of her palm and then asked, trying to smile, "Do you still write?"

She was making my insides quake. I felt my lips tremble and tried—with all the hurt of the world—to be honest in the simplest way possible.

"Yes."

She let out a deep sigh with a happy face. "I'm happy! Happy you held on to poetry. I think just writing poetry is heroic."

"It's the only thing holding me together now."

The silence stretched out. How could I tell her that I'd run away in order to write? Is it possible for something like that to be understood?

"Listen, Hayat . . ." I swallowed hard. "I ran away from my husband."

"What?"

"I ran away."

Third Phone Call

"HELLO?"

"Finally!"

"Finally?"

"You bought a new number?"

"How are you?"

"There was no need to get rid of your old number. You could have turned the phone off and controlled when people can call you. Like the owner of the grocery store when he hangs a sign on the door. Open. Closed. Problem solved! You should have consulted me."

"About my plans to leave you?"

"You're clearly incapable of appreciating detail."

"I'm learning."

"And am I really that bad? Or are you feeling regret and anger because you didn't run away from Saqr during those years, so you decided to run away from me? To score a victory over the wrong enemy. Over your husband."

"You're never going to understand."

"Never going to understand what?"

"That I'm trying to save what I can, what's left of me. A person the size of the knuckle on your finger."

"A person the size of my knuckle? You're right, Thumbelina, I don't understand a thing. I'll never understand you, and frankly I don't think that's my fault. Your complete lack of reason, your impossible moods and constant crabbiness. Even the way you talk, it isn't the way people talk. Would it be a problem if you tried to talk, for once, like a normal person? To put your finger on the problem and say 'This is my problem'?"

"You're free of all that now. You should be celebrating."

"Just tell me, what is it that I didn't give you? Because I'm tired of playing detective and all I can remember is that I was always trying to make you happy."

"Everything I say seems like hieroglyphics to you."

"Try me."

"Fine! If I put the lovely furniture and the wallpaper and your little gifts aside, you really aren't any different from Saqr."

"You can't be serious!"

"Think about it. You say: 'I don't want my wife to work. I don't approve of you studying. Everything you write must remain in the drawer. This is what you're going to wear and this is what you're going to think about.' I guess the rope around my neck was loosened a little but it's still here and I feel it and I can't tolerate it any longer."

"All I've done was exercise my legitimate rights."

"You're right. In the end no one will blame you if you act like a small god. You'll find the judge and the cleric on your side, and society puts its full weight behind your authority. I don't blame you. You've found sufficient arguments to lay claim to all of my rights! But I can't accept this either. I'm not obligated to be involved in a relationship of this kind. Not in a hundred years."

"You won't live a hundred years."

"I don't think I'm missing much, honestly."

"Why didn't you say that before?"

"Say what? Say 'Let me study please,' and kiss your hand and beg you to allow me to enjoy my natural rights as a human being, and call that generosity on your part?"

"I didn't think it was this serious. School, for example."

"School is just an example."

"What do you want?"

"Nothing. I want a divorce."

212

Partner in Crime

"IT'S NOT BAD." THAT'S WHAT Hayat said. "It's not bad. From outside it looks like a dump, but the room isn't so bad. How did you find it?" She was taking off her shoes and lying down on the bed, raising her legs and resting her heels against the wall.

"These shoes are horrible!"

She seemed to have forgotten I was there. Or I was just there to hear the sound of her thoughts. Then she turned to me and asked curiously, "How much a night?"

"Twenty-five dinars."

She did the math in her head then cried, "Seven hundred and fifty dinars a month!"

"You get a discount if you stay longer. I paid five hundred for a month."

"And you're broke now?"

"Pretty much."

"We'll get your money back. You can stay with me."

I wanted to ask her so many things. Does she have a husband, children? What does she do for a living? What happened during those years? But before I could, she said, "So, you ran away?"

"What can I get you to drink?"

"Water. Is he bad?"

"Who?"

"Your husband."

"In what sense?"

"In the sense that he's like Saqr, for example."

"No. And he's not bad in general. He doesn't drink, doesn't hit, he does what is expected of him. Overall he's a nice person."

"Then where's the problem?"

"He's not the problem. I am. I am no longer capable of playing by this world's rules. And I don't want to be forced to. I don't want to lie and scheme or beg and plead for my rights. I don't want to have a job because my husband 'allows' me to. I want to have a job because I want to. Here's your water."

She sat up, sitting cross-legged in the middle of the bed. I looked at her for a moment and my heart smiled. It was still her. Just like four years ago, the same energy.

"When did you decide?"

"After I started writing poetry again."

I was silent. It was that fateful moment. The moment that poetry materializes in my life not as an identity or talent or passion, but as a savior, an active force in my life. A partner in crime! For a woman to run away from her husband—who seems practically without fault—in order to write poetry. What a story!

"But why did you run away, Fatima? Why didn't you get a divorce like other women?"

"Because a divorce is his decision in the end, and I want to participate in this decision. I want to state my point of view. I had to. I had to—" I swallowed, shaking with emotion. "I had to do it for me! To get out of the tomb!"

Fourth Phone Call

"YOU DON'T UNDERSTAND! YOU NEVER understand! I'm trying to preserve what little fragile existence I have in this world. It's pointless for us to talk about any relationship in which one person is this worn down! You leave us to rust and rot and be killed, but still the relationship is sacred and must be respected! Marriage must be respected even if it harms someone. Everything that is not beating or cursing is not considered harmful in any way. Any discussion of the 'relationship' when one of the people in it is incapable of being themselves is merely an attempt to falsify and oversimplify reality. Writing saves me from all of that. When I write I am me. Why do you want to take that from me?"

"I didn't forbid you . . ."

"The drugs, the sleeping pills, the antidepressants, the migraines, the nightmares . . . What a heavy price you're making me pay in order to stop writing."

"There's no problem with you writing within the framework of the rules that I set out for you."

"The rules that my writing must remain in my drawers and notebooks! That I hide the scandal called 'Fatima,' the catastrophe called 'Fatima'! No, I won't do it. I won't write in tombs, no more tombs! No more!"

"We live in a small country. You know how people would receive something like this."

"No one can tolerate beauty."

"What garbage!"

"You can all tolerate ugliness, tolerate child abuse and rape, you can tolerate cursing and swearing, domestic violence, racism, you can tolerate Israel, America, your sectarianism, government corruption, underage marriage, everything! You can tolerate all the garbage in the world but you can't tolerate a poem."

"You could publish them under a pen name."

"No."

"I'm trying to accommodate you but you aren't trying, you're determined to reject every solution, you refuse to compromise!"

"There is no compromising on a principle. I don't see any difference between how I was buried alive in Saqr's basement and what you're doing when you read my poems with critical eyes, put its lines on trial and interrogate me about what I meant with this word and that expression. Then you lock the poem in your drawer and decide to 'allow' me—because you are kindhearted—to keep it. As long as I write for myself. In case you haven't noticed, I am wasting away in my loneliness and I want to enjoy a full life. I want to work, to get a degree, to write, and maybe volunteer for a civil rights organization and carry signs condemning Arab governments. I want to enjoy my life in full. Why does it have to be so difficult? Because I am a woman?"

Knives Flying

Thinking about you is like thinking about a dagger
    sunk into one's side.
Like thinking about the antidepressants that never
    work.
Like thinking about thirst instead of water.

A gentle executioner.
An affable judge.
A kindly jailer.

YOUR GENTLENESS . . . WHILE YOU PUT my hands in chains, place
the silence in my mouth, push the pins into my wrist. Shhh . . .
, you say. If you stay calm everything will be easier for both of
us. Shhh . . . , you say kindly, while your warm, sweaty hand
releases an odor of rust and iron, like a mask, over my face.
My facial expressions are indecent; no one wants my misery
to be exposed.

    You held me and patted my hair while your other hand
was busy inserting the needle, plotting a trap, poisoning a
dream. You hurt me with utmost tenderness, between many
kisses, in the endless desert expanse in your chest where I ran
for a long time. Yours was an exceptional way of offering me
pain and love together, until I no longer knew where the first
ended and when the second would begin, if it was possible to
distinguish between them at all.

You weren't crude or boorish. Your voice was warm like winter stores and your hand was light as a circus clown, while you moved from one instrument of torture to another, begging me to let things go. You apologized as you sank the pins into my heart, a kind nurse.

I was your plaything. I was the ideal victim, confusing hurt for pleasure, pain for love. My body trembled under your wing, soaring outside the logic of things. Where does your love begin and the harm you inflict end? Where does your hatred begin and your tenderness end?

My ability to love, to both give and receive it, stalled. My senses were crippled, along with my femininity, my intuition, my intelligence, and everything I might have been. I could no longer understand love outside the cries of my pain. The pain of your presence and the emptiness of your absence. All love was suspect, all tenderness was a trick, every cleaver, every knife, every whip one of love's faces. Your equivocal sadism cut me from inside. For every lashing I received from Saqr's iqal I used to become deeply familiar with ugliness. With you, ugliness was beautiful and beautiful things were ugly. You killed my ability to look at things. The world was one big suspicion, a crime scene operated by silk threads and soft gloves. And I—I was center stage, receiving the blows and the kisses, the love and the pain, not understanding a thing.

The first time I told you I wanted to go back to school, you answered without thinking, saying simply that there was no reason to. You decided just like that, paging through the morning newspaper in your military uniform, ready to go to work. I don't have the right to study. My eyes filled with tears. You promised to take me out for dinner. I didn't understand.

Months later I told you that I'd gotten tired of sitting at home. That I didn't have much to do. I told you I wanted to work. This time I was resting my head on your forearm on the long couch in the living room. We were watching a movie, *Déjà Vu* with Denzel Washington. I had my own déjà vu in turn.

No, you said simply, and sighed. Then you squeezed me closer to your chest and started talking about the dust hanging in the air-conditioning vents, and that if I was suffering from too much free time perhaps it was because I hadn't paid attention to the many things that could keep me busy here. Like the dust in the air-conditioning vents. Like the orange cake I hadn't perfected yet. Like polishing the candelabras. Like the millions of little things that circle in your orbit . . . master. Everything your eye might fall on must be perfect, from the way I wear my hair to the carved tomato flowers in the center of the salad bowl. That's fine, no problem. I can make tomato flowers and have a job, have a job doing anything. I could be a librarian, for example. And really I'm not interested in turning tomatoes into flowers. A tomato is a tomato and a flower is a flower and we couldn't be more insolent in our desire to ignore the true essence of things and force them to submit to our whims. But no matter, if the tomato flowers are so important to you I'll make them. You won't eat them and probably won't look at them for more than two seconds, yet if that's the price Your Excellency is asking I will make the effort and create more and more tomato flowers—but I want to work! I want to do something that belongs to me alone. Will you allow it? It's not possible. It's not allowed. You say it in a low voice, contented and happy: No. Then what do I do? I get up from the couch and slam the door in your face and lie down in bed. What do you do? You pick up a comb and comb my hair for me until I fall asleep. I rest my head on my defeat and the gentleness of your fingers and it becomes impossible to distinguish just when your fingers end and when my wound begins.

Two months ago, you found out that I write. You found out that I was born to write, that I'd written my whole life, and that I, in one way or another, had started writing again after Saqr had drained those waters from my heart. It had come back to me with a surprising fluidity, bursting from inside and running over. Language was being born in my guts. I was pregnant with poetry, and I wrote. But you—you stood in your military uniform, your hurried stance, inspecting the papers with your hands until the letters trembled as you scratched at them with your fingers.

"What's this?"

What a question.

"How long have you been writing?"

"I've always written."

"I've never seen you write before."

"I stopped for a while, started again recently."

"Started again?"

"Started writing again."

Yes, that's how it happened. Like sunstroke, like a bullet in the forehead, like a jolt of electricity to the brain, like stumbling in the middle of the street. It was an accident, a real accident. I was trying to buy half a sheep from the butcher and I . . . I had my feet firmly on the ground when the sky snatched me up and carried me far away. I told the butcher, I'm sorry, I'll come back later. It was hours before I came back. I searched for a place to hide. Writing must always be in secret, that's what Saqr's blows taught me. I went into a public restroom and took a pen out of my handbag, searched for a piece of paper, a napkin, a box of tissues! On the back of an old receipt I wrote the words that had started tearing through me again. I started writing again.

"What you write . . ."

You seemed to be having problems finding an appropriate way to finish. You coughed, scratched your forehead, tried.

"It's completely new."

"New?"

"I've never read anything like it. It's strange too."

"Thank you."

"Does it make you happy to write strange things?"

"'I am comfortable in the strangeness of words.'"

"Is that a joke?"

"Not at all."

"Do you mean you're happy because you write about 'the gazelle head fixed to the wall, the nails groaning from the weight,' and things like that?"

"Definitely."

"But that isn't what concerns me . . ."

"What concerns you?"

"That I can see you in the text. That scares me. Actually, it bothers me."

"Why does it bother you to see me?"

"It bothers me for others to see you. So . . . so clearly."

"What do you mean?"

"I mean . . ." He swallowed. "I'm happy that you've found a way to express yourself, with such freedom, but . . ."

"But?"

"But this writing isn't for publication. It would be scandalous."

"How can writing be scandalous?"

"Your pain, your fear, your terror. Do you really need to hang out all this dirty laundry for everyone to see?"

"My poems aren't dirty laundry."

"Don't argue with me."

"Words have no life without a reader!"

"Then don't write . . ."

"How can you say something like that?"

"Write if you want to, but don't think about publishing these poems. I forbid you."

The ideal husband. One who doesn't hit or yell or drink or cheat, who smokes occasionally, watches movies, doesn't ask much from his wife: just give up everything that might be attributed to her. The ideal husband, who investigates, forbids, and amputates with the greatest of compassion.

The circus can't go on. I can't stay like this, fixed to the wall waiting for the flying knives to land—with the force of mercy and mistake—on my forehead and finish me off. This suicidal act can't go on forever. So I decided. I left.

Carefully Folded Socks

"Okay, you're coming with me."

It was the day after we'd met. She stood there at the door of my room in her leather sandals and faded blue jeans, her sleeves carefully folded at the elbows, a smile on her lips. In her smile there was stubbornness, and in her stubbornness love. You're coming with me, Hayat said. Where? Home, Fatima.

She said it with a maternal tone, mixed with mild rebuke. She rushed into the room with long steps and headed toward the closet. She opened the doors, took out a knotted pile of sleeves and legs and socks, and occupied herself pulling a pant leg from the sleeve of a dress, untying a mismatched pair of socks, looking for the button that came off the gray shirt, as if the chaos that swept through my room like a flood wasn't cause for surprise or reproach. She gives her love with absolute mastery, while folding socks.

I followed her as instructed and started to gather the pieces scattered around the room, searching among the ruins of my heart after the bomb. The mirror is the mirror, my face is my face. The witch has disappeared, and the apple remained.

"This will stay here."

She was holding a package of alprazolam in her right hand, heading toward the garbage can, stepping on the pedal to open the cover. The garbage can opened its mouth hungrily, the saliva dripping from its teeth.

"I need my medication."

"This isn't medication. You get medication by prescription. Do you have a prescription?"

"I already told you . . ."

"You don't need this poison."

"I can't sleep without it."

"Then we'll sit up all night together."

The package fell from her hand, into the dragon's belly. Hayat was silent; my heart broke.

We latched the suitcases, gathered up the madness of the place. I put on my shoes and said to her, You go ahead.

I was thinking of the white package that pulls me gently from my reality, my medication that protects me from the world, vanquisher of epilepsy and depression and the only friend I had during the bad days and darkness. How would I leave it here, alone, to be devoured by the stomach acids of the iron dragon, along with the thousands of tissues and bad poetry.

"You don't need it, Fatima."

"You don't know the truth."

I wanted to add: We're in love and thinking of getting married. But before I could, she said, "Do you know what the problem is?"

"What?"

"The problem is that you're strong, but you think you're weak. You ran away and lived alone in this room—for a week, alone with your poems! Someone, a woman especially, would need supernatural strength to rent herself a room alone and fill it with poems. You don't need this drug, Fatima—you're out of the tomb. Anyone else would be happy to have a husband who confines her under layers and layers of black, to bear a dozen children and spend the day peeling truffles, but you. . . . You crossed through the gates of hell, and wrote many poems. They have taken nothing from you."

Andalusian Verse

WE GOT THE REST OF my money back from the hotel and left. We were crossing al-Khalij Street in the blue Peugeot and saw the sea fusing with the sky in a collusion of color, as if the sea had forgotten it was the sea and the sky had forgotten it was the sky, each of them lost in the other.

Hayat put a CD into the player, summoning Fairuz's voice.

"How's Faris?"

"He's no longer screaming into the phone."

"That's a good sign."

"He probably lost his voice—he screamed for five whole days."

"Maybe now he can try listening."

"He stays silent and listens to me for hours. He asked me about my poems, my childhood, about my mother and Saqr and what exactly happened to me in those days. He never asked about those things before."

"That's great, Fatima."

"Is it really great? I don't think it means anything, but it's becoming a habit. Why am I going into all these details with him when I'm declaring that our relationship is over?"

"Talking can never be bad. If renting a hotel room is what's going to push men to listen to us then we should all do like you."

"What's weird is that in our discussions I never feel that the person on the other end of the line is the man named

225

Faris I married a year ago, but is the whole society, the system, the rules, the lethal perpetuation of the unhealthy double standard. It's this world that I'm talking to, the one I recently declared myself to be different from and in disagreement with. I'm talking to it through my husband, my future ex. I talk to him and it's as if I'm trying to change things! To liberate freedom and limit harm. In the heat of the conversation I sometimes feel that my soul has risen above the scene. I'm seeing myself from a higher place and I laugh at the absurdity of the attempt. At Don Quixote tilting at the windmills inside me. It's a comedy!"

"You must be enjoying that."

"Are you kidding? I don't feel this power at all. And it's a power that comes from inside myself, without the need to impose any kind of control! I'm strong without hostility, strong because I am me. I hang up the phone and call him the next night for him to tell me that he didn't sleep because he was so busy thinking about what I said. I'm turning into a real pain. Even so, I sometimes feel that it's my inventive new way of destroying myself, to delve into a dialogue with the other to this extent, to go to the end of the tunnel despite knowing it's blocked at the other end. What's the point?"

We were silent for a few minutes. We let Fairuz's voice fill the space. We forgot ourselves in the Andalusian song woven from al-Mutanabbi's poetry: If you wish to kill me, you're the judge. Who can question a master about his slave? A sigh escaped from my chest, deep, drawn out from a faraway place. An unusual sigh, as if it was four years old, and as if it came out of a heart that was not mine.

"By the way," said Hayat, "Isam says hello."

Hayat's Life

HAYAT IS ME IN ANOTHER life. Hayat is me if I'd had a life.

Perhaps if I'd had a life like Hayat's, I would have been exactly like her.

It's like looking at a prettier version of yourself. This is what my life should have been like, had the accident not happened, had I not become an orphan, had there been no tomb or love or poetry or marriage or other things. With this stark simplicity: a woman with short hair, smile lines around the mouth that spread out when her face bursts into a smile, like a secret language. A white cotton shirt, faded blue jeans that are snug at the thighs and widen around the calf, a jacket irreverently belted at the waist, beige with a dark-brown satin lining. This would have been me, had my life not been stolen from me. I look at myself in my other rendition, in Hayat's life. I like what I see in myself when I am not me.

Hayat—who is me had it been possible to forestall the disaster—opens the doors of her home to me, shows me the secret locations of the coffee and sugar and dark chocolate, pushes a dish filled with cherries toward me, and introduces me to her husband Ahmad and her son Musayd. She was opening wide all the doors of her life for me, but the only thing filling my being and ruling my insides was pain.

Like an endless abyss of darkness and other things. Jealousy of Hayat, of her life, of the cheerful husband who creates traditional paintings and takes her to Zell am See in Austria every summer, the wonderful child occupied with his shiny red bike in the courtyard of the house, the volunteer work, the political activism, and many, many things, could have been mine, had I not . . .

"Do you like your room?"

She said it with eyes that penetrated the mask of my face. My features betrayed me.

"It's very nice."

My voice wavered and I cried. I sat on the edge of the bed and the soft, light-blue cotton blanket shot straight into my soul. The parquet floor smiled at me, a painting of the sea filled with sailboats extended their masts to me. It was a very blue room, and I cried from the blackness of my heart.

"It's not too late, Fatima."

"Forgive me."

"Forgive you for what?"

"The fire inside me."

She smiled. Pulled a chair over and sat in front of me while holding my wrists with firm hands.

"You're not dead yet, Fatima."

"They stole my life."

"I know."

"They stole everything."

"But you're here now, and you can enjoy your life in full. You can write, you can travel, you can love. As far as what you experienced, what you lived . . . the truth that was revealed to you alone, the frightening face of the world that you faced alone, this knowledge that you have inside you, that none of us have in us, believe me, my friend, we all envy you for it."

Fifth Phone Call

"IT'S BEEN TEN DAYS . . ."

"That's right."

"Ten days, Fatima!"

"I know."

"I miss you! I miss you a lot!"

"Did I tell you what I did yesterday for six hours?"

"What did you do?"

"I put my hands in my coat pockets and walked."

"For six hours?"

"Yes. I put my hands in my pockets and walked along al-Shuwaikh coast."

"Do you really have to say 'I put my hands in my pockets' as if there's some special meaning to it?"

"I love the look of a person with their hands in their pockets. A look of unconcern and liberation. It also tells you that I went out without a handbag. I'm relieving myself of everything. Lately I've been feeling that all the things that exist in the world simply out of habit annoy me and make me itch and scratch."

"So you walked for six hours. That's it?"

"Six hours, Faris! Six hours! I remember one time, it was a clear winter day and I wanted to walk to the grocery store. You acted as if I was about to bring on a scandal. I'll drive you, you said. I was unable to walk for ten minutes, and yesterday . . . yesterday I just walked, I walked for six hours, and there was the sea and the horizon and the oil tankers exporting petrol so that we can import it back again. That's a funny story. But what matters, Faris, is that I walked, for six hours, as if I were trying to catch up with what I'd missed out on. Then I wondered what those ten days of running away had done to me. I'm turning into a street cat. I explore the sidewalk and dig in the beaches and roam at night and I remember you. I think about your Dunhill cologne and your Adidas deodorant, the heat of your hand and the roughness of the sole of your foot when you rub it against my leg before you sleep. I remember the scent of your cigarettes and your shirt buttons, half of which are missing and half of which are still fastened, precisely like our marriage, and I feel for the first time in ten days that I love you."

"So . . . you're coming back?"

"No. I love you more when you're not around. Yesterday I decided to hold on to this love. I like it. I'm not saying that to convince you of the value of our marriage, but of the rightness of our divorce. Only thinking about divorce gives me a chance to see you like this, relieved of our relationship, and to have thoughts of missing you."

"You're talking like a crazy person again."

"You have no right to talk about me that way. What I'm saying makes sense; it just doesn't really resemble what the mothers and fathers and ancestors whose fists control our lives down to the last centimeter would say. If divorce is going to make me capable of love and smiling and walking for six hours . . . then it's the best thing that can happen to me."

"What about me? Do you think I'm going to call you up one day to enumerate the merits of divorce, extol its features and tell you it's the best thing that has happened in my life?"

"I can't stay in a marriage I don't want to be in out of pity."

"I think you have a duty to come back so we can solve our marital differences like grown-ups."

"You're wasting your time with me. You can be happier with another woman. And I . . . I'm very happy with my ability to remember the buttons on your shirt and your smile, and this is the most you're going to get from a woman like me."

"I don't want another woman. It's not that simple. You're acting like you're exchanging a shirt. I've gotten used to you and I like having you in my life, but it seems a poet like you can't appreciate these feelings."

"I'm trying to be fair, and to be fair to myself first of all. I can't give you anything, and you in turn can rob me of everything. I don't want you. I can't be your wife."

"I'm trying to come up with solutions while you're focused on destroying all possibilities of reconciliation."

"What about what *I* want? A divorce, anything! Why do you leave what I want out of the equation as if it doesn't mean anything to you? Did my desires ever mean anything to you? What about my desire to make my own decisions about things that affect me?"

"This is a technical matter. I'm your legal guardian."

"If this is marriage then I don't want it."

"But this *is* marriage, Fatima, and we can't change the world's rules."

"I don't want to change the world's rules. I don't want the world's rules to rob me of what I have left. As for you, I am certain you'll come across a thousand suitable women. I wish you luck."

"Wait . . ."

"Goodbye."

"Fatima, Saqr is sick."

"What did you say?"

"He lost his vision in one eye. He wants you to visit him."

"Saqr lost his vision?"

"It's the diabetes."

Life 101

"ARE YOU SURE?"

"Yes."

"We can go back now if you don't feel like it."

"It's fine. I want to do this."

She smiled and the lines at the corners of her mouth spread out. I smiled too, my half-smile.

"Let's go then," said Ahmad. "I'll come with you, in case something happens."

What could happen? Anything can happen to anyone. That's Life 101. We got out of the car and crossed through the long marble hallway, passing through the depths of Amiri Hospital. The smell of cigarettes lingered everywhere. We went up to the Men's Internal Medicine wing. I met Wadha in the corridor. She hurried to meet me.

"How's your father?"

"He lost his right eye."

"When did that happen?"

"Three days ago. He's screaming from the pain in his stomach." Then she added, looking deep into my eyes, "He asked for you twice."

"I hope he feels better soon."

Why did Saqr bother to ask about me now? She gave my blue summery dress an examining look and couldn't help but comment.

"Your husband allows you to go out without an abaya?"

"That's none of his business."

"How's that?"

"That's none of your business."

"You married a liberal guy! I knew it the first time I saw him."

"Are you going to keep jabbering on like this?"

"Who are they?" She motioned her head toward Hayat and Ahmad standing three meters away from us. "Where's your husband?"

"This is my friend Hayat and her husband Ahmad."

She pursed her lips and said reservedly, "Pleased to meet you." She meant the opposite.

Badriya came out of the room and hugged me while letting out a deep sigh, "God brought you!"

"How are you, Badriya?"

"I'm fine. You look great! We've missed you! How are you?"

"Fine."

"Saqr asked for you twice."

"I heard."

"He'd love to see you. He's been asking about you since he lost his eye."

That's it then. He wants to see me for the last time before he loses his left eye too. He wants to see where I ended up. As his creature, his monstrosity. He wants to know what his efforts accomplished.

"You can go in, Fatima."

Yes, I'll go in, into the dragon's lair for the last time.

"I Saw Nothing but Beauty"

ONE STEP INTO THE CAVE.

"Who is it? Who's there?"

"Me."

I saw him. A pile of bones called my older brother. White gauze covered his right eye. There were white tubes in his veins, a white dry patch on his mouth, a white beard, white scalp, white bedsheet. He was barely breathing. Is this the dragon that guarded my tomb?

"Fatima?"

"Yes."

"So you came?"

"Yes."

"You decided to remember your older brother who raised you and looked after you?"

I smiled. "How could I forget?"

"You haven't visited us since you got married! We haven't seen you since Eid al-Adha last year. When did you decide to cut off your family? Aren't you familiar with the verse: '*Then, is it to be expected of you, if ye were put in authority, that ye will do mischief in the land, and break your ties of kith and kin?*'"

I smiled and recited the next verse, "'*Such are the men whom Allah has cursed for He has made them deaf and blinded their sight.*'"

My voice was encased in a surprising sonority, and his face started to quiver.

"Did you come to gloat over my misfortune, my blindness?"

"No."

"You were always ill-natured and hard-hearted."

"When you look at me, you see the reflection of your own true nature."

"And what do you see in me?"

"'A man for whom one eye is enough.'"

"You're gloating over your brother, your brother who raised you . . ."

"Never."

"Why did you come?"

"Why did you ask for me?"

"Why did you accept?"

"To tell you a few things."

"What things?"

I took a deep breath. "I came to tell you that I forgive you."

His cheek quivered. "Forgive me for what?"

I swallowed. This time my voice shook as I spoke; it came out patchy, with a muffled sob. After all these years he's going to deny what he did to me?

"You hurt me a lot, and you know that."

"I did my job."

"What job? That of a jailer?"

"The job of a guardian."

"A guardian who beats me with his iqal and slaps me with his shoe."

"You were wrong, and the wrongful must be punished."

"By being placed under house arrest for three years?"

"That was to protect you. You were sliding down unsafe paths. Poetry readings and male colleagues and God knows what else."

"I was in love."

"You dare to say it to my face!"

"I was in love with Isam!"

"Damn you and your bad manners!"

He turned away from me. I saw that he was weak.

"I could have married a man who loved me, but you weren't going to allow that. You weren't going to allow me to have anything that made me happy, not love, not poetry. And when you got tired of having me in your house you threw me to Faris."

"You married Faris out of your own free will."

I took a step closer. I sat on the chair to his right, looking into his one eye.

"Tell me. . . . What are you going to do after you die, if you meet God and find yourself accused of insulting Him?"

"I'm not the one who needs to worry here."

"How do you know?"

"I read the Quran and the Sunnah and I don't take my creed from poets!"

"You put thousands of barriers between me and God, you monopolized God for yourself, and all those years you repeated that I was sinful and inadequate and bad . . ."

"I was trying to wake you up. Don't blame me for your weak faith."

"In the end I am your creation. The fruit of seven years in prison, three of them in solitary. Your crimes against me, you committed them in the name of God alone. You can't wash your hands of your responsibility to me so easily. That's why you asked to see me . . ." I exhaled. "Don't worry, I forgive you."

"I didn't do anything wrong to warrant forgiveness."

"You don't deserve forgiveness but I am giving it to you because I deserve it. I want to live the rest of my life without constantly wondering: why did that happen to me? Why did you hurt me so much? Why do you hate me?"

"I didn't . . ."

"I forgive you. I forgive you, Saqr. Believe me, 'I saw nothing but beauty.'"

237

"I don't want to talk anymore. Let me rest."

"You don't have to say anything. You can rest now and stop asking for me and summoning me. You can also stop repeating that garbage about cutting off your family. I didn't cut anyone off—you stomped all over our family ties with your shoe. There's no need to hide behind that beard because I can see you very well from where I'm at."

"Get out of my room!"

"I'll leave. I'll leave with open arms because my life will begin as soon as I leave you. I will divorce Faris, I will work as a journalist, I will write many poems. I have my life back and you didn't win."

This Poet of Yours

"WHY DID YOU RUN AWAY?"

I was in the kitchen with Hayat, making a fruit salad. Hayat was beating eggs because Ahmad wanted balaleet for dinner. Musayd was playing with his ninja turtles on the white ceramic floor. It was a normal life, a nice life. I was living at Hayat's house and it was like being in the heart of the world. Musayd calls me "Aunt Fatima." I'm his aunt, a sister, an organic part of this place. I have a family.

I was preoccupied with pulling grapes from the bunch and tossing them into the bowl.

"Why did you run away, Fatima?"

Her question caught me off guard.

"What do you mean?"

"You know exactly what I'm talking about."

Her glance went through me and she read my thoughts so well I felt embarrassed. I averted my eyes.

"I don't want to get into it," I mumbled.

"Coward."

She said it with that mocking tone. After all these years, she was still doing her job provoking me.

"Shut up!" I said, throwing a grape at her.

She caught it in her hand and tossed it into her month, laughing. I didn't laugh. I grabbed the knife and sank it into an apple: open-heart surgery. My body burned hot under the cotton shirt.

"Ask me about him. I know you want to know how he's doing."

I moaned. "What's the point?"

"What do you mean?"

"It's been four years. Neither of us are the same."

"No harm in asking."

"Fine!"

I pulled the knife out of the apple, then plunged it back in anxiously.

"Did he get married?"

"No."

The mountain moved from my chest and the weight dissipated. I smiled. "No?"

"No."

Hayat laughed. She laughed at the rapid shift in my expression.

I put the knife and the apple down. My voice softened. "What does he do?"

"Arabic teacher."

"Really?"

"He's still in the writers' group."

"Does he write?"

"He didn't stop."

"Has he published anything?"

"Some poems. In *al-Qabas*, *al-Rai*, and *Asharq al-Awsat*. I saved all of them."

"A book?"

"Not yet."

"What else?"

"He wants to see you."

My mouth went dry. My body shook. I was bold and asked, my question terrifying: "Does he know I got married?"

"He'd expected as much."

"Did you tell him?"

"The whole story."

"When?"

"After we met the first time, you and me. I met him and told him about you."

"What did he say?"

"He didn't say anything. He just looked at me in that way, as if he wanted to draw every word out of my mouth."

"That's everything? He didn't say anything at all?"

"He said, 'When can I see her?'"

I smiled again, and it wasn't a half-smile. Hayat smiled. Existence expanded in her smile, expanded like a smile. The world is broad and arched.

"What are you trying to say?"

"He's called twelve times since you moved here. He sends forty messages a minute. He's a real pain, this poet of yours."

Failure to Comply

THE DOORBELL RANG. THEY'D FINALLY arrived.

We went out to receive him. He seemed tense, with clenched fists. A strange man was with him.

"Hello Faris. Please come in."

Faris frowned. "Who are you?"

"This is Ahmad," I interrupted. "My friend Hayat's husband."

"Pleased to meet you," he said with a frown. He crossed the threshold with rushed steps; I smiled at him and didn't ask how he was. He looked like he was about to blow up in my face.

"You're still smiling?"

"Are you okay?"

"Horrible. You?"

I was embarrassed to say "Fine," so I kept quiet. He grabbed my blouse with his fingers. "Where's your abaya?" he whispered, nearly hissing.

I laughed. He was clinging to his illusions of control to the last, this man.

"Who's he?" I asked.

"Mr. Abu Riyad, attorney."

"You brought a lawyer?"

"And you brought them . . ."

"They're friends."

"Bad influences."

Ahmad invited everyone to come in. He opened the door and led the two men to the living room. Hayat had made some tea and sat close to me. She was giving me all of her strength.

Faris sat next to his lawyer and looked at me with his profound eyes.

"Won't you serve me some tea?"

I smiled cheerfully. Everything this husband did to convince himself that he held absolute authority made me feel my strength. I got up from my place and gave him and Abu Riyad some tea. It was silent for a couple of minutes. Ahmad resumed the conversation.

"Thank you for accepting the invitation, Faris. I hope we can reach final a solution to the problem. Fatima here . . ."

"Don't speak for my wife. You have no legal capacity in this matter. We should have met at my house or at her family's house, but thanks to her stubbornness . . ."

"Meet you at your house so you can lock me inside and put an end to the problem?" My question spilled from my mouth, inflammatory and hot. "You can't hurt me in Ahmad's house."

"Just so you know, I'm not Saqr. It seems you're still confused about that. Maybe you've forgotten to take your medication."

Hayat interrupted. "Fatima was taking alprazolam without a prescription and you encouraged her to continue?"

"First, Fatima is ill. Second, this is none of your business."

I interrupted: "You're insulting them in their home."

"You're the one who started with the insults. If it weren't for you we wouldn't be here. In their home."

"Everyone!" Abu Riyad cut us off. "I suggest we stop quarreling over secondary matters and discuss the heart of the problem."

Ahmad nodded.

Abu Riyad continued: "What I understand from my client is that his wife, Fatima, has been absent from the marital home for two weeks and refuses to return."

"That's correct," I confirmed.

"I'm here today to tell Fatima that my client is prepared to file a case against her for failure to comply with her duty of obedience to her husband if she doesn't return with him to the marital home today."

Failure to comply. Very nice, that expression.

"According to my knowledge of the law," Ahmad said, "which is of course very limited, sir, Faris can file this case and can establish his wife's disobedience, but he can't enforce the ruling. In short, no one has the right to force Fatima to return to the marital home against her will."

"That's correct, but this also means she will lose all her marital rights."

"He can keep the money," I commented, crossing one leg over the other. Then I looked at Faris and added, "I could have filed for a divorce for damages from the beginning. I didn't. I was hoping we'd reach a mutual agreement to divorce."

"I am not in agreement!" cried Faris. "I am not asking you for anything other than my rights as your husband. Far from it."

"I don't want to be your wife, so don't talk to me about the rights tied up with that."

"You became my wife and that's that."

"By a scratch-and-win card."

He pointed at me and yelled, "By a trap! A trap planted by your brother's wife. She told my family that you were the perfect girl for me. Doesn't study, doesn't work, doesn't want much. After we got married, surprise! I find out she wants to study and work—turns out she's a poet too! That's just what I needed, I swear!"

"It was a mistake from the beginning, then. Correct it and divorce me."

He went off like a gun. "This is a scandal! Everyone is asking about you and I don't know what to say. 'She's busy, she traveled, she's wandering around Dubai's shopping malls, she's visiting her family in Bahrain. . . .' Every day I lie to cover up your recklessness in hopes that you'll come back to your senses, come back to your home! The neighbors are asking about your missing car, my mother scolds me because I visit her alone! My sisters are inundating me with questions. Every day that goes by the scandal gets bigger. I don't deserve all this. I'm a nice man and a good husband. I've been patient with you and your illnesses and pills and medications and infertility and frigidity. I've been patient and faithful to you, and you leave home like this, you run away like a coward. . . ."

"You're right. I'm infertile and sick and crazy and frigid and disobedient. You have all the grounds required to divorce me without anyone blaming you for it."

"I don't understand. Why are you talking about divorce as if we're talking about buying bread?"

"I want one."

"I don't."

"You want a woman who doesn't want you?"

"My wife doesn't know what she wants. She's crazy."

"There's nothing wrong with her," interjected Hayat, with her excessive motherliness. She couldn't keep herself from saying something.

"Divorce me, Faris," I continued. "I divorced you fourteen days ago."

"Women cannot divorce," Abu Riyad commented. "Women must petition a judge to grant a khula releasing the wife from the marriage for pecuniary compensation."

The expression shone in my mind: khula! Like someone stumbling upon an emergency exit. Pull to release.

"How much?"

"For what?"

"A khula. How much?"

"Are you kidding?"

"No."

"Where would you get the money anyway?"

"I'll take out a loan. I have a salary and I can take out a loan. I'll give you back all your dinars. Every dinar you paid to Saqr to acquire ownership of me, believing that it's your right to dictate what my life should be like. If you don't divorce me I will seek a khula."

His features looked troubled and his face trembled. "Are you serious, Fatima?"

For a moment I felt sorry for him. I wanted to pat him on the shoulder and assuage his fear. I sighed deeply. "Could we have some time alone?" I asked.

"Of course," said Ahmad, turning to the attorney. "Come along, sir, let's take a walk in the garden."

Hayat whispered that she'd be nearby.

That Memory

THE RED IN HIS EYES pained my heart.

"Listen, Faris . . ." I sighed.

But he didn't listen. He was lost in a daze.

"You'd seek a khula?"

"Listen, please."

"Am I a pair of pants?"

"Don't talk about yourself like that, Faris."

"You'd just get rid of me like that?"

I gathered my courage. Got up from my chair and sat on his right. I clasped his palm and squeezed it.

"Divorce would be better for you. If you get remarried you won't be bothered by a khula case. It would be easier for you. It wouldn't seem like there's something wrong with you. You know how people talk, how people see these things . . ."

"Now you're thinking about what's best for me?"

"I don't hate you."

"Do you love me?"

I smiled. Squeezed his palm between my hands. "Not enough to be your wife."

"What do you want us to be?"

"Friends?"

"That doesn't make any sense. Plus, it's wrong."

He makes me smile, this son of righteous society. "Then nothing," I continued. "We'll be that memory."

"What memory?"

"The one you remember and smile at without regret. I want to be that memory."

He smiled and bowed his head. For the first time I felt that the idea of divorce had penetrated his mind. It had been hovering around him like a moth for two weeks. Now it was inside him, swaying heavily.

"If the divorce takes place at the request of the wife, she loses her right to alimony."

What an awful expression. Alimony in Arabic is *nafaqat al-muta*: roughly, 'pleasure compensation.' Sounds like he's being asked to pay for having 'enjoyed' me.

I smiled. Then he smiled.

"You know, I really loved you," he said.

I patted his shoulder. "You really think you loved me?"

"Shame on you for doubting it."

"Think about it. You loved what you thought I was. You loved the Fatima that Badriya painted for you. A girl who doesn't want much. A housewife who lives to sculpt flowers out of tomatoes. That's not me. It's what you want me to be but it's not me."

"I liked your strange ideas sometimes."

"Really?"

"Sometimes . . ."

We smiled. We were drifting on a wild current taking us right up to the end, except now, for the first time, he was allowing things to happen and not paddling against the current. He took a deep breath.

"Are you sure this is what you want?"

"Yes."

He withdrew his hand from mine, stood up. I looked at him from the chair before him. He looked out of reach and taller than usual. He gave me a farewell look.

"Goodbye, dear."

"Goodbye." My heart beat like mad.

"I divorce you."

My whole body went weak. Divorce, no matter how much we may want it, hurts. I wanted to cry but didn't.

"Tomorrow I'll go to the court and register the divorce."

"Thank you."

It was over. He turned his back to me, opened the door and started to leave.

"Goodbye, Fatima."

"Goodbye, Faris."

The Guest

I slipped off my shirt and lay on my stomach on top of the cotton bedspread in my room. This was one of the habits I'd started since I began working at the paper. Every day, at three in the afternoon, I lie down on my bed in my bare skin and embrace it. I say to it, I'm home, darling! You're so nice and cool! I rest my cheek on its chest and close my eyes.

"Aunt Fatima?"

Musayd was knocking on the door. I put on my shirt and called to him.

"Come in, Musayd."

"Mama wants to know when you're coming. She says the world might end if Papa goes hungry any longer."

I laughed. "I'll come down right away and save the world."

"Mama says that Papa turns into the Incredible Hulk when he's hungry."

"Your mama has a strong imagination."

He reaches out his right hand and grabs mine, his stuffed lion in his left hand. We go downstairs together. We open the door and enter the living room together. I stumble and go back out, alone.

The gasp nearly swallows me whole. I rest my back against the wall in the hallway, confused. Is it him?

This face, this half face, a vertical slice of a long story, the nose, the eyebrow, the forehead, the hand resting on the mouth and the leg crossed over a leg, why hasn't he changed in four years?

Hayat jumped up from her chair and hurried over to me.

"What's wrong?"

"You're asking me what's wrong?"

"That was my question, yes."

"Is it him?"

"Yes, it's him."

"What is he doing here?"

"He was invited."

"Are you playing pranks on me now?"

"Don't blow things out of proportion."

My hand jerked. I trembled, my body shaking like a reed. My eyes filled with tears.

"Did he see me?" I asked.

"I think so . . ."

"What if after all this time I don't love him?"

"You don't have to."

"What if he doesn't love me?"

"Doesn't matter."

My knees went weak and I covered my face with my palm. My voice came out hoarse: "How could you do this to me?"

"You want to see him but you're too afraid to do it."

"You've started making decisions for me?"

I looked at her, standing in front of me. She looked strong and impervious. She was unbearable.

"I told you I don't want to see him!" I yelled.

"I don't believe that garbage."

"You have no right . . ."

"You're just meeting someone, Fatima. Just meeting an old friend. That's all."

She sat on the ground in front of me, holding my forearms, which were folded over my face. She looked deep into my eyes.

"Your excuses are no good anymore," she said in a decisive tone. "Not Saqr, not Faris, not the tomb. You no longer have anything to hide behind."

"How could you do this to me?"

"You'll thank me later."

"We'll argue about this later!" I yelled and walked away, her voice following me.

"You can't run away from life, Fatima!"

Of course I can. I can run away from life, I can run away from everything. I know all about running away. She'll see. She'll regret it.

I went out into the street, headed toward my car, then remembered the keys were in my room. I cursed and swore. I have to get out of here. I have to.

I turned around to go back.

He was behind me.

He stood there like an exclamation point. Tense as a question.

It was him, the poet.

"Does everything have to be difficult with you?"

His old voice reached me, spread under my skin. He was handsome in his white shirt. My heart raced and my mouth went dry. I turned away.

He came a step closer, his voice soft and his question merciless.

"Aren't you going to say something nice?"

My eyes filled with tears.

"'Good evening.' 'How are you.' 'Nice to see you.' Things like that," he continued. "Can you give me something like that?"

The words inside me were tied around my feet.

My mouth was a stubborn knot.

I am a tear.

"You could say other nice things. 'The end of the world.' 'The crushing force of nonexistence,' things like that . . ."

"I . . ."

"Make things easier for me!"

How? How could I make them easier for him? How could I make them easier for me? How is it possible to get past all that history? The poetry reading. The slap. The poem buried in my throat, the thread of blood, the shame, the chair that flew in the air . . .

"Were you hurt?"

"Sorry?"

"That day. The chair he threw at you . . ."

"You're worried about that chair?"

"I just want to know."

"A small bruise on the arm."

"You were okay."

For a moment it seemed there was nothing to say. I thought it was the perfect moment for a new escape, but I didn't do it. I didn't run.

"Aren't you going to say anything else?"

"I didn't want to see you."

"You're mad at me?"

"No."

"I'm mad at me. I haven't forgiven myself for a moment."

"It wasn't your fault."

"Of course it was. You suffered a lot because of me."

"I wanted that. I wanted love and poetry and experience. The slaps too. I wanted him to slap me so that I could hate him."

"You could have been killed . . ."

"I think a part of me wanted to die too."

"I'm sorry, Fatima."

"Is that why you came? To ask for forgiveness?"

"Part of me. Another part wanted . . ."

"The other part?"

"Just to see you."

"I didn't want to see you."

"You've said that twice."

I felt his heart sink in grief. He grimaced and turned to leave.

I opened my mouth, snatched the ends of the threads to the words from a far-off place. I'll say something nice. I'll move past my wounds and say something nice to this poet.

"You seem well."

He turned back around, seemed happy with the thin thread that I was extending to continue the conversation. He rubbed his head with his right hand and stammered, "I've gained weight and lost the rest of my hair."

"True."

"You're very beautiful."

Chills rippled under my skin.

"And you fold up into yourself . . ."

"Like a map?"

"I am a sailor."

We smiled.

The memory was still alive. It made me smile.

"Hey, you two!" Hayat was calling from the living room window. "We're starving! The world might end if . . ."

We exchanged glances and smiled. Things had gotten easier. Talking was easier, smiling was easier, looking too.

"Feed your husband, Hayat. We'll stay here. We have some things to talk about."

I sat and he sat, under the old lotus tree. A man, a woman, and poetry makes three. The memory comes and forgetfulness recedes. I smile at him and he smiles at me, friends.

"Tell me, please," he said, sitting up in his seat. "Are you still writing?"

"I'm writing like a madwoman."

"Does this mean you'll publish your first collection of poetry soon?"

"My first novel."

"A novel? Have you started writing novels?"

"Writing one novel. One novel is enough."

"What is it about?"

"The same old story."

The same old story: a man and a woman, a lot of memories and a little forgetfulness, with the exception that the hero of the story isn't the man or the woman or memory or forgetfulness.

It's poetry.

Notes

The quotations on the pages below are by the following writers (in order of appearance). Translations are the translator's own, unless otherwise noted.

p vii. J. Krishnamurti, *Krishnamurti's Notebook*, (March 7th), 379. © 2003 Krishnamurti Foundation Trust Ltd., Brockwood Park, Bramdean, Hampshire SO24 0LQ, England. Content reproduced with permission. Permission to quote from the works of J. Krishnamurti or other works for which the copyright is held by the Krishnamurti Foundation of America or the Krishnamurti Foundation Trust Ltd has been given on the understanding that such permission does not indicate endorsement of the views expressed in this publication. For more information about J. Krishnamurti (1895–1986) please see: www.jkrishnamurti.org; p vii. Malik Ibn al-Rayb, line from the poem "Malik Ibn al-Rayb yarthi nafsahu" in which the poet mourns his own death; pp 4–5. Badr Shakir al-Sayyab, lines from "Sifr Ayyub" [The book of Job] and "Unshudat al-matar" [Rain song]; p 23. Title of a novel by Ismail Fahd Ismail, *Ba'idan ila huna* [Far away to here]; p 84. *The Quran*, 26: 224, 3: 113, translated by Abdulla Yusuf Ali; p 119. Badr Shakir al-Sayyab, "Unshudat al-matar" [Rain song]; p 119. Fragment of poetry by Tamim ibn Muqbil; p 123. George Orwell, *1984* (New York: Harcourt, Inc., 1949), 89; p 126. Fragment of poetry by al-Bakhrazi; p 127. Ibn Hazm, *The Ring of the Dove: A Treatise on the Art and Practice of Arab Love*, trans. A.J. Arberry

(London, Luzac & Company, LTD: 1953), 21; p 132. Lines from a poem originally written in French by: Rainer Maria Rilke, *Roses*, trans. David Need (Durham, NC: Horse & Buggy Press, 2014); p 137. Fragment of poetry by al-Muthaqqib al-Abdi; p 152. Line from a song by Muhammad Adib al-Da-yikh, line of poetry by Qays Ibn al-Mulawwah, line from the mu'allaqa of Tarafah ibn al-'Abd, line by Abul 'Ala Al-Ma'arri; p 152. Fragments of poetry: by al-Marqash al-Asghar, from the mu'allaqa of Imru' al-Qays, by Abu Khirash al-Hathli, by al-Akhtal, and by al-Farazdaq; p 158. Lines from an anec-dote attributed to Al-Asma'i; p 166. Souad al-Sabah, "Laylat al-qabd 'ala Fatima" [The night Fatima was arrested]; p 178. Orwell, *1984*, 342; p 194. Muzaffar al-Nawab, "Watariyat lay-aliya" [Night strings] (twice); p 220. Line inspired by one from Qassim Hadad, "Kitabat al-hilm" [Writing a dream] in Tarfeh bin al-Wardeh; p 235. *The Quran*, 47: 22–23, translated by Abdulla Yusuf Ali; p 236. Line from a short story by Ghassan Kanafani, "Nasf al-'alim" [Half the world]; p 237. Statement attributed to Zaynab bint 'Ali bin Abi Taleb, from her speech before the Caliph Yazid.